THE SECRET LIFE OF
OWEN SKYE

THE SECRET LIFE OF OWEN SKYE

ALAN CUMYN

A GROUNDWOOD BOOK

DOUGLAS & McINTYRE

TORONTO VANCOUVER BERKELEY

Groundwood Books / Douglas & McIntyre
720 Bathurst Street, Suite 500, Toronto, Ontario M5S 2R4

Distributed in the USA by Publishers Group West
1700 Fourth Street, Berkeley, CA 94710

We acknowledge for their financial support of our publishing
program the Canada Council for the Arts, the Ontario Arts
Council and the Government of Canada through the Book
Publishing Industry Development Program (BPIDP).

ONTARIO ARTS COUNCIL

National Library of Canada Cataloguing in Publication Data
Cumyn, Alan
The Secret Life of Owen Skye / Alan Cumyn.
ISBN 0-88899-506-7 (bound).
ISBN 0-88899-517-2 (pbk.)
I. Title.
PS8555.U489S42 2002 jC813'.54 C2002-902328-9 PZ7
Library of Congress Control Number: 2002106835

Cover illustration by Elsa Myotte
Design by Michael Solomon
Printed and bound in Canada

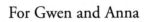

For Gwen and Anna

TABLE OF CONTENTS

FIRE AND RAIN

THERE was a brass jar on the mantle above the fireplace in the old falling-down farmhouse where Owen Skye lived with his family years ago. Horace, Owen's father, kept the jar polished and gleaming. It had belonged to Owen's grandfather, who was now dead, and so it seemed to have special powers.

Owen's grandfather had been a sailor, and the brass jar had gone with him all around the world. If Owen held it close to his nose, he thought he could smell a thousand different places. But the lid of the jar was jammed on so tight that only the strongest individuals could open it. Even Owen's older brother Andy wasn't able to budge it, and he was terrifically strong.

Of course Leonard, the youngest brother, couldn't open it, either. He was too small and weak. Besides, he wore glasses, which tended to fall off if he tried too hard at anything.

The jar rattled whenever you shook it. No one knew what was in there: gold coins perhaps, or emeralds, or dried pirate bones. Owen rarely passed by the mantle without pulling the jar down, grasping the brass knob and yanking as hard as he could. No matter how hard he tried, the top wouldn't come off.

Horace was an insurance salesman. But he didn't sell a lot of insurance except to himself, which was why they were living in the falling-down farmhouse. Horace convinced his wife Margaret to buy the house because it looked like it would topple in the first high wind. Then the insurance company would pay them enough money to build a brand-new house. Owen and his brothers would race around like wild horses and kick chunks out of the walls trying to make the house fall down. It slouched anyway, and the roof sagged like an old bed that's mostly been slept in in the middle.

One day in early September Margaret gave a bridge party. For days beforehand she cleaned the house and tried to keep the three boys from messing everything up again. On the afternoon of the party she was busy running back and forth to the kitchen getting tea and coffee and wedges of cake and cheese biscuits and Jell-O with marshmallows in it, and talking to all the other ladies.

Andy and Leonard were busy stealing sugar cubes from the delicate glass bowl that their mother only brought down from the highest cupboard for special occasions. They would stroll past the bowl on the table, humming quietly, and pull off the top with all the silence and swiftness of secret agents. Then they would dart a sugar cube, and maybe even a second, into their mouths.

Owen liked sugar cubes too, but after the first couple he thought he would try once again to open the brass jar. He wanted it to be a secret. He wanted to take the jar away and open it all by himself and then show his brothers the treasure inside.

It wasn't difficult to slip away, since his brothers were hovering like hornets around the sugar bowl and his mother was so distracted looking after the details of her party.

Owen took the brass jar to a safe hiding spot, underneath the front porch. He grabbed the knob with his right hand and held the base of the jar between his sneakers and pulled. When that didn't work he took the knob with both hands and pulled so hard his shoes slid and he fell against a beam and smacked his head.

Owen went back inside holding his head.

"I want you to keep your grubby fingers out of the sugar bowl, do you hear?" Margaret said to him.

Owen said that he would. He went to the kitchen. Andy and Leonard were washing their hands in the sink and didn't see him slip a ball of twine out of the utility drawer.

Owen went back outside and took the brass jar and the twine to the apple tree in the backyard. He tied the twine around one of the lower branches and then fastened it to the brass knob using a bowline, which his father had taught him. A bowline knot never slips no matter how hard you yank. Owen yanked terrifically hard and the knot held.

But the string broke. So he doubled up the string and re-tied the knot and yanked and yanked until the double string broke as well.

After that Owen quadrupled the string and pulled so hard the branch swayed, but the lid stayed on.

His brothers were going to come out any minute. Owen could feel it. Andy would say, "What are you doing?" and then he'd take over. He always did, because he was so tall and strong and had such wild ideas for things to do. Owen was skinny and his ears stuck out and he almost always did what Andy said. But this time he wanted it to be his idea. So he thought, what would Andy do to get this top off?

Owen cut the brass jar down from the lower branch with his pocket knife. Then he took the jar and climbed as high as he could get in the tree. He quadrupled the twine again and carefully tied one end around the brass knob and the other around a stout limb that was far enough out to be clear of other branches underneath.

Andy and Leonard were going to come out any second. Owen knew it. And he so wanted to be able to show them the vials of dried vampire's blood and other treasures. So he gripped the brass jar as hard as he could and leaped off the branch.

He fell down, down. He felt the jerk of the twine pulling tight, the bend of the branch. Then his body snapped like a whip, and he couldn't tell where he was or what was happening.

The next thing he knew he was on the ground, on his back, and the tree was way above him, dark branches and leaves and scrawny apples against gray clouds. The base of the jar was still in his hands but the lid was dangling in the sky, suspended by the twine.

It didn't hurt at all, until Owen realized how far he'd fallen, and then it did hurt, but not too badly.

The ground was littered with little boxes. They all said the same thing: *BRYANT & MAY'S, British Made, Special Safety Matches.*

Owen collected them all quickly and put them back in the jar. Then he climbed the tree and cut down the lid and took it all back to his hiding spot under the stairs. Andy and Leonard came out but they didn't see him, and then they went inside again.

Many times Margaret and Horace had told the boys never to play with matches. But these were so old, Owen wasn't sure they would light. He took one of the boxes and opened it, and drew out a single, crooked match. It looked a hundred years old. Then he struck it against the sandpaper side of the box.

Nothing.

So he tried another one, and another, and finally there was a bad smell and then the match lit and the fire started burning toward his fingers.

Owen dropped the match onto some old dead leaves and in a moment the leaves were burning. He quickly kicked on some dirt and stepped on the fire with his sneaker.

After that Owen was so relieved he almost put the matches back in the container. He could have burned down the whole house! He knew that his father was hoping for the house to fall down in a disaster so that they could get a new house with the insurance. But maybe a fire wouldn't count for the insurance company, which was very particular about what kind of disaster it was.

So to keep from burning down the house, Owen went out to the ditch and squatted in the tall grass and took out the matches again.

The grass was taller than Owen and dry and hard despite all the rain that summer. Owen started just a little fire, a tiny one with a few twigs. The flames spread slowly and gently and turned the twigs into glowing, curling little pieces. Then they became black and the glow went on to other twigs.

At that moment a little bit of wind came up. The glow went from the twigs to the tall, dry grass, and before he knew it, Owen was surrounded by a wall of flame! It happened so fast he hardly had time to think.

Owen ran through a hole in the flames and hid under the front porch and held his breath for ten seconds. Then he peeked out and saw that the wall of flame was heading straight for the house!

Owen ran into the house to tell his mother. But by then Margaret was sitting with her friends and they were all talking so loud that Owen had the feeling he couldn't possibly explain.

So he just stood in the middle of the room and yelled, "Look out the window!"

He couldn't bring himself to say *Fire!* He was too ashamed of what he'd done. And he couldn't look himself. He just sat down where he was and put his hands over his eyes.

"Mom! Over there!" Andy yelled. Then all the ladies got up and went to the window. They said things like, "Look at that!" and "Well, isn't *that* something." And after awhile they went back to their bridge game.

Margaret touched Owen's shoulder and said sweetly, "I think you can open your eyes now."

So Owen went over to the window and looked out in amazement at near-darkness and slashing rain. It was one of those instant thunderstorms that blow up every now and again. Andy and Leonard were glued to the glass to watch every lightning bolt. Owen stared at the black smudge in the ditch where the tall grass used to be, and he tried to think how it could have happened that in his exact moment of crisis he'd been saved.

One of the ladies remembered that she'd left the windows open in her car, so Owen volunteered to go out and close them. He got soaked in just a few seconds. On his way back he ducked under the front porch and returned all the matchboxes to the brass jar. He stuffed the lid on so tight he hoped it would never be opened again. Then he snuck the jar back into the house and returned it to the mantle, dried himself off, and waited for his father to come home.

Owen was certain his father would see the burnt grass in the ditch and know exactly what had happened. Then Horace would go to the cupboard in the kitchen and take out the warped ruler that he used for disciplining the boys.

Horace had told them many times about the ruler. He had stolen it when he was in grade three, and had kept it all these years as a reminder of how important it was to stay straight in life. Most of the lines and numbers had worn off and really it was only good for one thing anymore.

But when Horace got home the rain was still falling so hard and fast it seemed to be hitting the house like ocean waves. If he did notice the smudge in the ditch, he didn't say anything.

By then the bridge ladies had gone home and Margaret and the boys were running around like crazy with pots trying to catch all the leaks in the roof. The boys' attic bedroom was the worst. There was a terrible leak right over the big bed where the boys slept. Margaret had brought up the corn pot to put on the bed, and that's exactly where Horace fell through the roof when he went up in the storm with a bucket of tar to try to fix the leak.

Luckily Horace didn't fall all the way. Just his foot and leg went through. Owen looked up in wonder at the wiggling leg. Little bits of wood splinter and shingle and spurts of rain were falling down onto the bed. Then Horace's boot came off and shot across the room. It bounced off the dresser and left a tarry print.

Margaret yelled up at her husband to get his leg out of the ceiling, but he couldn't. He was wedged in tight at the thigh, with his other leg splayed across the roof at an awkward angle. He couldn't push himself up. The rain was pouring down and he said some things only reserved for the most difficult moments.

While their mother was yelling up instructions, Owen was thinking it was all his fault. If he hadn't opened the jar and started the fire then the rain wouldn't have come so hard and so fast. He knew by now this all had something to do with his dead grandfather, whose spirit must have been trapped in the jar, and who must have brought the rain to try to protect them. But now there was too much rain and Horace was trapped. It was all because of Owen.

"We need to get a hammer," he said.

"What? To hammer his leg out?" Andy said. He could corkscrew his voice to make anything sound ridiculous.

"No. To hammer a bigger hole in the ceiling."

"But the hammer's down in the basement," Leonard said.

The basement was the darkest, scariest part of that old farmhouse. There was no door to it from inside. You had to go outside to the old, creaky double doors of the coal chute. And there were no lights. It smelled of mold, and water dripping down limestone, and in the corners there were snakes, and rats, and worse.

"I'll go," Owen said weakly. It was the thought of the fire that made him say it. What if he did nothing brave and important to make up for causing this disaster?

"We'll all go," Andy insisted.

Outside, the rain was slashing down harder than ever. Owen's Indian Brave flashlight worked for only a few seconds in the moisture, then went dark. The boys carried on anyway. They went in through the coal chute, sliding down on the seats of their trousers. It was so black and cold and creepy that Owen could hardly breathe.

"Shhh!" Andy said, and they froze in the darkness.

"What is it?" Leonard asked. He started crying before Andy could answer.

"It's nothing. Just the wind." But the way Andy said it made it sound like it could be the Bog Man.

The Bog Man had been stealing cattle all summer. At night he came out of the bog by the Ridge Road and slimed across the fields making slow gurgling noises. Then he chose the weakest of the cows — a calf, preferably, but he was strong enough to bring down a bull — and squeezed it by the neck with his long Bog Man fingers, injecting poison through his fingernails until the cow's bones were soup. Finally he would sink his terrible teeth into the base of the skull and drink out the animal, brain first, leaving only a shriveled sack of cowhide in the morning.

If the Bog Man got you there was no escape. It was better to just hold your breath and hope that he ate you quickly.

Leonard turned and ran up the coal chute screaming. Owen tried to turn and run, but his feet wouldn't move. Then Andy took a few more steps into the gloom.

"Andy — be careful!" Owen said. There was a

gurgling noise then. It sounded like it was coming from the blackness underneath the work bench.

Andy didn't say anything, which was exactly what happened when the Bog Man got you. Those long Bog Man fingers choked the words right out of you. Owen wondered whether he should try to save his big brother or run away and save himself.

Horace had told them that if you stand up to bullies they'll run away — most of the time. So Owen wondered if maybe the Bog Man was like a bully, and if he jumped on top of him then maybe the Bog Man would be so surprised he'd let go of Andy for a moment and forget about injecting the poison.

But Owen also knew the Bog Man was mostly made of bog, which was something you sank into like quicksand and never got out of. The more you struggled the worse it got. You sank and sank until your legs were covered, then your waist. If you held up your hands to keep them free, that just made you sink faster — *right into the Bog Man.*

"Andy?" Owen said, but there was more silence and he knew he should run, because now the Bog Man knew where he was. Owen turned around but everything was black. He couldn't remember which way he'd come in. He heard more gurgling and tried to think what to do.

Then the Bog Man put a slimy hand on Owen's shoulder. Owen screamed right in his face. It was too dark to see anything, but the scream did the trick, because Andy managed to escape then too and ran straight into Owen. The two of them fell over, then got up so fast the Bog Man didn't have a chance. Andy found the coal chute and they ran all the way out.

They had completely forgotten the hammer. But it didn't matter because Horace had managed to pull his leg out on his own. He wasn't hurt, but the hole was still there. And the bed was soaked.

They pushed the bed into the corner, and Margaret put the big corn pot in the middle of the room to catch the rain that was now pouring in.

The hole stayed in their bedroom roof for some days before Horace hired a man to plug it up properly. Owen loved to lie in bed and look up at the stars, to see possibilities where there had only been wood before. He thought a lot about his grandfather, of all the places the brass jar had sailed to around the world, and how nice it was that there might be a special spirit looking out for him. And he was able to forgive himself for almost burning down the house, because he'd had the courage to try to save his father by facing the Bog Man. He didn't tell anyone for the longest time, but kept it kindling inside him like a small fire that was all his own.

THE BOG MAN'S WIFE

THERE was a haunted house near the Skyes' farmhouse. It was in the woods beside the bull's field, and because it was haunted it was completely deserted.

No one knew why the deserted house was in the middle of the woods. Trees hadn't been cleared, except where the building was. The front door was nailed shut but the window beside it was easy to climb through, and the sign warning people away had fallen down and had moss over it.

The house had never been finished. Inside they had to climb the beams to get to the second floor, and the walls were open. They could look from room to room and see where the electrical wires were supposed to go, the pipes and the furnace vents. Owen found a doorknob on the floor and Andy found a bone-handled knife with a rusty blade that he oiled and sharpened back into shape. Leonard found a clawhammer with one broken prong. There were rusty nails lying around, and odd bits of wood.

And right in the middle of what was going to be the living room sat a red couch.

There was something secret and scary about the red couch. Every time they visited, it looked like someone had been sitting in it. That's how they knew the house was haunted, and why they would only go during the day and never stay long.

Weeks passed, the days grew colder, and then it was Halloween. Owen was the family superhero Doom Monkey the Unpredictable, Andy was Frankenstein, and Leonard was a Living Corpse. It was the first Halloween they were allowed to go out by themselves, if they stayed together, and Andy thought they should do something terrifying so they would remember it. Owen thought that was a great idea. But Leonard was scared. He didn't even like going to the haunted house in the daytime.

Leonard finally agreed to go if Andy gave him all his chocolate bars and took Leonard's unshelled peanuts. They made the exchange on the road and then Leonard insisted on eating two of his chocolate bars right away.

He finished them, then had a third, but was still scared.

"I'll wait here while you guys go!"

"Come on!" Andy said. "You agreed! You took my chocolate bars!"

Leonard did his best to get out of it, but the chocolate was on his face and he had to go. He whimpered along the path in the woods to the haunted house. Andy was in front with Owen's Indian Brave flashlight, which was working again, though the batteries were low. Leonard was in the middle so he couldn't run away.

It was a cold night and the darkness in the woods was almost as deep as the darkness in the basement. Leonard held onto Andy's chainlink Frankenstein belt until they were going so slowly that Andy turned around and shone the light straight into Leonard's eyes.

"Don't!" Leonard said.

"Well, hurry up!" said Andy. "You're just making it more scary!"

The house looked like one big black shadow. Andy shone the flashlight on it but they couldn't see much in the weak light. Owen had been reading a lot in bed at night and had spent his allowance on comics instead of new batteries, so now when the boys really needed a good light they were in trouble. But they had come all that way so they couldn't back out.

"I just want to have a look at the couch," Andy said. "If there *is* a ghost, it probably sits on the couch at night."

"Why do we have to see?" Leonard said.

"It could be the Bog Man," Owen said. He thought probably the Bog Man would like a dry place to sleep every now and again.

"I've been thinking about this ghost," Andy said, and he squatted down and turned off Owen's flashlight to preserve the batteries.

"What?" Leonard asked. They all squatted beside Andy and kept their voices low.

"There was an old story," Andy said, "that the Bog Man had a wife."

"A wife!" Leonard said, too loud, almost laughing.

Andy and Owen said, "Shhh!"

"What would the Bog Man need a *wife* for?" Leonard laughed. "To clean the swamp? Iron his boggy shirts? Fold his moldy socks?"

"Is that what you think a wife is for?" Andy asked quietly, and Leonard stopped laughing.

"There's more," Leonard said, but in a little voice.

"Oh, yeah?" said Andy. "What else is a wife for?"

Leonard thought a long time. "Dishes."

"What about babies?" Andy asked

"Yes," said Leonard.

"Yes, what?" Andy's voice was sharp.

"Men can have babies too," Leonard blurted.

"No!" Andy said, and this time Owen had to "Shhh!" him down too. Then Andy's voice became friendlier. "That's just it. You have to have a wife if you want to have a baby. Men can do all those other things without women. We can cook and clean and iron and sew and whatever you like. We can just learn it. But men can't learn how to have babies. It's never been done!"

"So girls are smarter than us?" Leonard asked. It seemed impossible to admit.

"There *are* things women can't do," Andy said strongly. Then it got quiet while he tried to think of them.

"Sure there are," Owen said. "Women can't fix radiators." He said that because the car radiator had broken and their father had to take it to a garage where the person who fixed it was a man.

"Women could learn that," Leonard said.

"But they'd have to get their hands dirty," Andy said, but in a weak voice. Just that week their mother had gotten her hands completely dirty fixing the plumbing under the kitchen sink. She could probably learn how to fix radiators in ten minutes.

"Women can't stickhandle," Andy said then.

"What about Sheila?" Owen asked. Sheila was the little girl in figure skates who scored all the goals for the Riverdale Hornets.

"She's got a good *shot*," Andy conceded. "But she's not a terrific stickhandler." He didn't seem so sure though.

"Maybe if we studied hard," Owen said, "if we spent a lot of time around girls, then we could figure out how to have babies."

"Spend time around girls!" Andy hooted. "What a stupid idea!"

"We could ask Mom!" said Leonard, but Andy shook his head. "Women never tell," he said. "I asked Dad, and he just laughed and said ask your mother. So I asked her but she wouldn't tell me. It's a big secret."

He stood up then and switched on the Indian Brave flashlight. The beam was weak.

"What about the Bog Man's wife?" Leonard asked. So Andy squatted down again and told the story.

The Bog Man used to be a nuclear biologist at a secret government lab underground. One day when he was mixing acid and plutonium there was a terrible explosion. The scientist barely survived, and wandered in the middle of the night into the bog, where he collapsed. Most of his skin had been burnt off in the explosion, but the cool waters and black moss of the bog soothed him. Because of the plutonium he absorbed natural radiation from the surrounding bog minerals, and so now was able to live forever. However, he had to eat one body every twenty-four hours to keep up his strength.

One day he thought he'd want a child. Of course, being a man, he didn't know how to make one, so he needed to find a wife. No woman was able to look at him without being paralyzed by fear. Desperate, he went to the orphange and stole a blind woman whose father had married his own cousin.

"It's lucky she didn't have two heads," Andy said. "Everyone knows you can't marry your own cousin."

She liked him well enough, but thought that he smelled boggy. Also, she wanted to live in a regular house, since the bog was so wet and froze over in the wintertime. Because she was so kind to him the Bog Man agreed to build her a house in the woods. He worked on it by himself, stealing the materials from lumber yards, using his extraordinary strength to dig the foundation, raise the walls, carry the roof beams. But just as he was getting close to finishing, she started to get ill. The radiation that gave him his eternal energy was killing her. He brought in the red couch so that she'd have something to sit on while he worked on the house. But she died before he could finish, so he abandoned the house to go live in the bog again.

When Andy was through telling the story, Leonard and Owen were quiet for a long time. Then Leonard asked, "Did she tell him how to make a baby before she died?"

"No."

"You'd think she would have told him," Leonard said. "Since she loved him, and she was dying anyway, and he'd never find another wife."

"I don't think she did love him," Andy said.

"She thought she loved him for awhile, then she got angry at him for making her sick. So she must have decided not to tell him in the end."

"It wasn't his fault he made her sick," Owen said. "He didn't know."

Andy stood up then and flicked on the flashlight. "We only have a couple of minutes to have a look," he said. The light was pretty feeble. "I just want to see if she's on the couch. She won't be able to see us," he added, "because she's blind."

"But she'll be able to hear us," Leonard said.

"Come on!" said Andy, and when he said it like that you had to follow. He could have led snowmen on a march into summertime.

They slipped through the window beside the boarded-up front door, then stood still, barely breathing, while Andy shone the weak light into the house.

"Do you see anything?" Leonard asked.

"Not sure," said Andy. He took a step forward and listened.

"What is it?" Owen asked.

"Shhh!" said Andy.

The light started to flicker. Then it died.

"Let's go!" said Leonard, who turned around

to go back to the window. But Andy caught him by his Living Corpse costume.

"We have to stick together," he whispered.

"Why?" Leonard asked.

"Shhh!"

Andy took a few more steps. There was a full moon shining through one of the windows. It wasn't shining directly on the couch but beside it, so that the couch itself was cast in deep shadows.

"See anything?" Owen asked.

"I'm not sure," Andy said. He took several steps forward. Leonard and Owen stayed back near the window.

"Andy?" called Owen.

"Shhh!" said Andy. "I think — "

Then there was a loud crash and Andy cried out. Leonard and Owen grabbed each other and screamed and huddled back against the wall.

Then silence.

Owen said, "Andy?"

Nothing.

"Andy? Are you all right?"

They heard someone whimpering in the darkness.

"You wait here," Owen said to Leonard. "If

anything happens to me, go home and get help."
Leonard nodded grimly. Owen stepped forward.

"Andy? Can you hear me?"

Nothing.

More steps.

"Andy?"

There was a low moan. Owen stopped, tried to see in the blackness. He could just make out the outline of the couch. There was something funny about it, something extra black. He stepped forward again.

"I'm here," Andy said. *"Don't — "*

Too late. Owen had already stepped into the hole where Andy had fallen through the floor. And Leonard, who hadn't stayed back like he was supposed to, landed on top of both of them.

"Ow!" said Leonard, shaking his hand. "I've got a splinter!"

"Stop crying about it!" said Andy. "I think my leg is broken!" His leg was very sore where he'd fallen on it, and the Indian Brave flashlight was crushed in his pocket. Bit by bit he brought out the pieces, which Owen could barely make out in the gloom. The situation was so serious that Owen forgave him. Instead he turned on Leonard.

"You were supposed to go get help!" Owen said.

"We have to get out of here," Andy said. He got his brothers to lift him, one under each shoulder. Then the three of them, hugging each other, slowly walked around the basement trying to find some stairs. They had never investigated that part of the house before, and weren't even sure there *were* stairs.

Leonard started to cry. So they sat down on the basement floor near the hole they had fallen through and ate candies from their sacks.

Owen couldn't help thinking about what he thought he'd seen up there on the couch. It was small and shadowy, but just might have been…

"I don't think there are any stairs," said Andy. "We'll have to go back up through the hole we made coming down."

"It's close to the couch," said Owen.

"She's already heard us," Andy said. "*If* she's there at all."

"You didn't see — ?"

"I'm not sure what I saw."

They ate bubblegum and licorice, suckers and candy kisses and caramel popcorn. They chewed as quietly as they could but every chomp sounded to Owen as loud as a hammer banging on a pot.

"She might have gone back," Owen said.

"What?"

"To get the Bog Man."

Andy stayed quiet for a moment. "We'd better get going!" he said.

Owen and Leonard stood and helped Andy up. Then they all looked at the hole above their heads. Normally Andy would climb up first and help the others out, but he couldn't with his broken leg. So it was Owen's responsibility. But when Leonard tried to boost him, they both fell over.

"You're going to have to boost Leonard up," Andy said.

"I'm not going first!" said Leonard.

"You have to! There's nobody else!"

"Forget it!" said Leonard. The only way they could get him to do it was if Owen agreed to give Leonard all his remaining chocolate bars and Owen would have to take the apples and raisins. Then Leonard wouldn't go until he'd eaten four more chocolate bars.

"When you get up there," Andy said, "look

around for a rope or a long stick or something to help us get out."

Owen boosted Leonard so hard that he shot out of the hole, then disappeared.

"Leonard?" Andy called. "Are you all right?"

Leonard didn't say anything.

"You might have thrown him too far," Andy said to Owen.

They called out again and finally Leonard said, "I see something!"

"What? What is it?"

"Shhhh!" Leonard said. They could hear his footsteps on the thin floor above them. The footsteps stopped for a moment, walked on, stopped again.

They could hear Leonard's little voice. "Who are you?" he asked.

There was no answer. Leonard took a step forward, then a step back. "Are you a ghost?" he asked.

Silence.

Leonard said, "I'm sorry about the Bog Man. Andy told me. This would have been a nice home for you."

Leonard shuffled his feet. Then he said, "Do

you like candy?" Andy and Owen didn't hear a reply. But they did hear a faint sound of unwrapping. There were chewing noises for a couple of minutes.

Leonard said, "My brothers are stuck down in the basement. I have to find a ladder for them. But there was something I wanted to ask you first." Owen couldn't believe that little Leonard was standing there talking to a ghost! But Leonard's voice was calm and normal and strangely polite.

"What I wanted to ask you," said Leonard, "since you're a woman. Or you used to be a woman. Is how you make babies? I was hoping to be the first boy to have one."

There was silence — except for some more chewing noises — for the longest time. Andy and Owen strained to listen to what she was saying, but it was very faint — like the whisper of the wind, or the scratch of a branch against a pane of glass.

Finally Leonard said, "Oh, I see. Well, thank you very much. And I'm very sorry for your tragedy."

He walked across the floor then, quickly, as if

it was daylight, and in a moment lowered a funny kind of ladder down the hole. It had been hammered together out of leftover lumber, but Owen and Andy had never seen it lying around the haunted house before. Andy went up first and Owen pushed him from behind.

As soon as they got up, they looked around but Leonard said, "She's gone now."

"You saw her? You saw the Bog Man's wife?"

"I saw her shadow," Leonard said.

"We heard you talking to her. We couldn't hear anything she said."

"You couldn't?" said Leonard.

"We just heard *you!*" said Owen. They were looking around at all the shadows. Any one of them could have been the Bog Man's wife.

"We'd better get home," said Leonard.

They helped Andy across the floor, then up and out of the window. It was truly a night for miracles, because the farther they got from the house, the better Andy's leg felt, so that by the time they were on the road again it wasn't broken anymore. Andy made his brothers swear an oath of secrecy to not tell their parents about the haunted house, because if they found out, the boys would never be allowed out on Halloween again.

Just before they got home, Andy stopped Leonard and said, "What did the Bog Man's wife say when you asked her how to make a baby?"

Leonard said he wouldn't tell them unless they handed over all the candies they had left. They argued and shouted but Leonard wouldn't be moved. So finally they dumped their bags into his and he filled his mouth with candy rockets and chocolate peanuts.

"Come on, a deal's a deal!" Andy said.

Leonard chewed slowly. He suddenly seemed to be a lot older.

"Please, Leonard!" Andy said finally. "What did she say? How do you make a baby?"

"It's a secret. She wouldn't tell me," Leonard said, wiping his mouth. "'Cause I'm a boy." And he ran inside the house before his brothers could touch him.

VALENTINE'S DAY

O WEN had the most private and terrible secret. He was in love — with a girl, of all things. Her name was Sylvia.

On the first day of school, when the kids chose the seat that would be theirs for the entire year, Owen watched where Sylvia sat. Then he headed for the opposite corner, as far away as he could get. But as soon as the desk was his he knew he had made a terrible mistake. He sat staring at her, wishing his desk closer. For days and weeks he imagined an airplane suddenly falling out of the sky, rushing at a thousand miles an hour straight into the windows of the classroom. While all the other kids ran for the door he'd flash across and tackle Sylvia under a desk so that the plane crash would just miss the both of them. Everybody else would be killed, so she'd have to marry him.

It was not a nice school. The principal was as tall as a beanpole and bald on top except for some gray curly hairs that came straight out of his ears, and red hairs bursting from his nose. His name was Mr. Schneider. Most of the time the kids never saw him. They only heard how mean he was. Everyone knew that if you were sent to Mr. Schneider, he made you stand by his big black desk in the office and bend over. Then he took out the Strap. If you cried he gave you an extra whack. Mr. Schneider was so old there was pretty well only one thing left in the world that he could do well.

The teachers got their kids so jittery with stories of Mr. Schneider and the Strap that as soon as the teacher left the classroom, somebody would jump up on a desk and yell out, "Don't do anything, or you'll get the Strap!"

Then someone else would jump up on a desk and scream, "But you're already doing something! He's going to give us *all* the Strap!" And then nearly everybody would be up on their desks, yelling and fighting, and someone would yell, *"Shhhh! Someone's coming! It's Mr. Schneider!"*

Then they'd all crash down from their desks and sit up straight in their chairs with their hands folded, holding their breath. And the footsteps would go *click click click* down the hall. If nobody looked in, there would be this terrible moment of silence when everyone knew they should just keep sitting there with their hands folded. But how could they? It was inhuman. First one kid would breathe and then another and before they knew it those kids would be up on their desks again, dancing and screaming.

At recess time they ran screaming from one end of the schoolyard to the other and back again. The girls chased the boys and kissed them if they caught them. The girls were bigger than the boys. There was a white line painted across the schoolyard to keep the girls from chasing the boys, but it didn't work. The girls took one look at that line and then ran right over it. And the teachers didn't care. They stayed in the staff room smoking at recess time. You could see the smoke puffing out of the window even though it was closed and the drapes were drawn. Those teachers didn't want anything to do with the kids at recess. Sometimes they forgot to ring the bell and the girls would chase and kiss boys for hours.

But Sylvia never chased. That was part of what was so impossible about her. Owen saw her once when he was walking back from a hockey game at night with Andy. It was wintertime by then, cold and black, and their footsteps made *crunch crunch* noises in the packed snow. They carried their hockey sticks and skates over their shoulders and walked silently in single file, cutting through the schoolyard on their way back from the rink.

Owen happened to look up at just the right moment. There was a light on in one of the class-rooms where some kids were taking piano lessons. One little girl looked up just as Owen was passing by. She had long pale blonde hair and blonde eye-lashes, and skin so soft it felt heavenly just to look at it. Her eyes were blue with light speckles, like the summer sky made into a jewel.

That was Sylvia. She lifted her eyes from the music book and looked directly at him as he walked past the window. It was a second and a half in a very bright light.

There's a funny thing about windows at night. When the lights are so bright inside, then outside people can see in perfectly. But the inside people only see a black window, with a reflection of themselves. Sylvia never saw Owen, though he didn't know that until much later, when he'd taken out this memory and examined it from every angle. But that night he felt like he'd pushed his finger into a light socket and given himself an electric shock. He was doomed.

On Valentine's Day all the kids had heart-shaped cardboard mailboxes taped to their desks. If you wanted to give somebody a Valentine you had to walk up and slip it in. Owen didn't want anybody to think that he was hopelessly in love with Sylvia, so he made cards for everyone in the class. When it came time to make Sylvia's card his hand shook with nervousness and it became difficult to breathe.

Owen wasn't a good cardmaker anyway. He had a hard time coloring inside the lines, and he wasn't good at spelling. He didn't know how to spell Sylvia. He spelled Dear and Love and his own name perfectly, but instead of starting Sylvia with an S, he started it with a C because he knew sometimes C could sound like an S and maybe this was one of those times. Then he walked around to everybody's heart-shaped mailbox and put in the cards.

When he got near Sylvia's he could barely make his feet move, and his face was a burning tomato. Just as he was putting the card in her box he read her name and noticed that it started with an S instead of a C. But it seemed to him impossible to stop putting the card in since he was there already and his arm had started moving and she was sitting right beside her box and if she turned and looked at him from such a close range he might die instantly. So he shoved it in, then rushed back to his seat and thought about what Sylvia sounded like if it started with a C. If you thought it was a soft C then it would just be Sylvia, the same. But if you thought it was a hard C then it became Kill-via, which might send the wrong message.

He had to get the card back. But how could he just walk up and put his hand in her heart-box and pull it out again? How could he be sure it was the right one? Her box was bulging with cards. She would take them out at three o'clock and read them one by one, then get to the one from Owen and his life would be over.

Owen rose to his feet. All the kids were back at their desks now because it was time for quiet reading. You weren't supposed to be walking around anymore.

The teacher was writing something on the blackboard, her back turned to the class. She was a lumpy, gray-haired woman named Mrs. Harridan, and she hated children.

Owen stepped toward Sylvia's desk. It was all the way across the classroom. The other kids started whispering but Owen couldn't stop. His feet were moving and his brain had stopped thinking. No danger seemed too great. He had to get that card back!

When he got to Sylvia's mailbox, Sylvia turned to him and said, "What are you doing?" Those were her first words directly spoken to him, even though he had saved her from countless plane crashes. Mrs. Harridan turned around and Owen thrust his hand into Sylvia's heart-box. He tried to grab the card near the top, but somehow all of them came bursting out and spilled on the floor. A staple broke on the side of her box as well, and part of the lace trim came off.

"Owen Skye!" Mrs. Harridan yelled. The classroom became completely silent.

Owen didn't know what he was doing any-more. Every card he looked at had Sylvia spelled correctly. He picked them up by bunches and tried to stuff them back in, but more staples gave way and now the heart-box was in tatters.

All the kids started laughing except for Sylvia, whose face was flaming. She had such delicate skin anyway, and was so quiet. He knew that to have everybody laughing like that was the worst thing imaginable.

As he was floundering with all her cards, Owen tried to say, "I'm sorry," but the sounds came out more like, *"Sworry."*

Mrs. Harridan sent Owen to the principal, Mr. Schneider. He had to walk, by himself, down the hallway past three classrooms, then turn right and go up the stairs. Everyone knew where the principal's office was but it was like the Bog Man had captured Owen and turned his brain to soup. He went down the hallway and turned right but nothing looked familiar. He'd never been in the hallway when it was completely empty like that. He went past class after class of kids sitting in rows and teachers talking with pointers in their hands.

Finally, when he knew he was lost and would never reach Mr. Schneider's office, he found it. He stood trembling in front of the big brown wooden door and knocked. Then he waited. His face and ears were still blazing red and everything seemed to be spinning slowly around him.

There was no answer. He knocked again, louder, and heard footsteps coming to the door. *Click click click.*

It was Mrs. Lime, the principal's secretary. She had big shoulders and small eyes and wore glasses with a black strap to keep them from falling down.

"Yes?" she said.

"I have… I am… uh… " Owen said.

"Have you been sent to see Mr. Schneider?" she asked.

"Yes, ma'am."

"What did you do?"

Owen had to think hard how to say what he'd done in just a few words. Finally he said, "I made a spelling mistake."

Mrs. Lime nodded, then told him to sit in one of the black chairs outside the door of Mr. Schneider's real office, which was inside the secretary's office. Owen sat with his back straight and his feet almost reaching the floor. For the first time he noticed that he was clutching a Valentine's card that had been in Sylvia's heart-box before he destroyed it. It wasn't his card, though. It was from Michael Baylor, and it said, "I loev you."

Owen read it over and over. So Michael Baylor was in love with her too! It was terrible to think about. When that plane came tumbling out of the sky there would be two of them rushing over to save Sylvia. And Michael Baylor sat a lot closer, so what was the point? Owen would probably arrive just in time to be hit by the landing gear.

Mr. Schneider came out of his office. He was even taller than usual, and his gray suit smelled of old cigarettes. He looked down from the clouds at Owen and said, "What is your name?"

Owen stood up, cleared his throat and said, "Michael Baylor."

"Well, now, Michael Baylor. What have you done?"

Owen told him the whole story. He told him how he was in love with Sylvia but had made a spelling mistake on her card and so went over to try to correct it even though he should have been sitting in his seat since it was quiet reading time. He didn't leave out any details. In fact, being Michael Baylor seemed to give him a reckless kind of courage. He finished up by saying, "You can give me the Strap if you like. I deserve it!"

Mr. Schneider scratched the hair in his ears and his nose. Then he cleared his throat. His face was grim.

But before he could speak, Mrs. Lime said from her desk, "It's Valentine's Day, sir." And Mr. Schneider said that he must promise not to make any kind of commotion again and Owen said no, sir, he wouldn't. Then Mr. Schneider sent him back to the classroom.

Owen walked in with his shoulders back and his head up. He pretended to sit down gently so all the kids would think he'd had the Strap. There were whispers up and down the rows but Owen looked unconcerned. He opened his notebook and wrote line after line — LOVE LOVE LOVE — getting the V and the E in the right order, just like Michael Baylor couldn't. He did not look at Sylvia and Sylvia did not look at him, and when he got home he threw Michael Baylor's card in the garbage and didn't tell anyone about it.

DOOM MONKEY THE
UNPREDICTABLE

ONE day that winter Uncle Lorne came to stay. He was Horace's unmarried brother. Margaret always used to say to Horace, "Look what would have happened to you if you hadn't married me!"

Uncle Lorne was as tall as the house practically and just barely skin and bones, because he'd been cooking for himself so long. He had a hard time finding clothes that fit, and didn't seem to care much anyway. His feet were huge, and his pants usually stopped several inches above his ankles. His shirt sleeves were often ripped and his ties always showed old dinner stains.

He was very shy, even with the kids. He'd be reading the newspaper in the kitchen after work, and when one of the boys came roaring around the corner, chasing Doom Monkey the Unpredictable, Uncle Lorne would rise up suddenly as if he'd been caught in the bathroom with his pants around his ankles. If someone said, "Hi,

Uncle Lorne!" he'd turn away and go back to the little cot in the basement that Horace had set up for him. Margaret hated that cot and often asked Uncle Lorne to use the pull-out couch in the living room. But he preferred to stay down in the gloom despite the possibility of encountering the Bog Man. He rigged up a light and built stairs to the kitchen, put down some plywood on the floor, and said it felt like home.

No one knew when Doom Monkey the Unpredictable was going to appear. Right in the middle of almost anything there might be a sudden cry: *This is a job for Doom Monkey!* Then there would be a race into the bedroom to get Doom Monkey's Atrocious Hat. It was made of brown velvet with lots of stuffing. Whoever put it on became Doom Monkey the Unpredictable, the trickiest fighter in the Western Hemisphere.

One time Doom Monkey was desperately needed to stop an invasion of space lizards. Andy grabbed the Atrocious Hat first, so Owen and Leonard were lizards. They screamed at the top of their lungs and scampered around the house. Just as Andy was corralling them, he lost the Atrocious Hat and Owen became Doom Monkey.

At this point the lizards took over and Doom Monkey's mission was to somehow survive. He raced into the closet in the attic bedroom and brought down an avalanche of clothes on top of the pursuing lizards. Then he sped downstairs and across the living room and ducked behind the old green sofa. The lizards thought he was in the kitchen. He slipped out the front door, ran in his shoes through the snow to the coal chute and into the basement, which wasn't as scary as it used to be since Uncle Lorne had fixed it up a bit.

Owen crept under Uncle Lorne's cot.

There wasn't as much room there as Owen had thought there would be. The space was filled with magazines — thick, glossy ones full of pictures of old cars. There were gleaming Fords and Hudsons and little French racing cars that looked like torpedoes on wheels. Almost all the cars had beautiful women lying on top of them, or bending over to rub the headlights, or looking in the mirrors to check their lipstick. Owen had never seen so many pictures of beautiful women. The Atrocious Hat fell off him while he was huddled under the cot looking. It was hard to see in the shadows.

He was so engrossed in the pictures that he forgot about everything.

Suddenly the new basement light went on. Owen looked over and saw a huge pair of boots beside the cot. Then he screamed and scrambled out. He slipped on the magazines, ripping some of the pages. He ran straight into the little bedside bench and knocked over the water dish that held Uncle Lorne's spare set of false teeth.

"Hey!" Uncle Lorne said, and straightened up to grab for him, but bonked his head on a low beam and fell over.

Just then Andy and Leonard came down the stairs to the scene of disaster. The kids didn't know what to do with Uncle Lorne. He was knocked out, and the beam had left a big square bruise on his forehead. And he was too big to lift or even drag back to the cot. Andy poured the remaining false tooth water over Lorne's face.

That made Uncle Lorne sit up, sudden as a mummy, and the boys ran away. Lorne never said anything about it, and even the bruise on his forehead faded after awhile.

In secret, talking in low voices so that the boys had to be quiet to hear, Margaret and Horace would discuss what to do with Uncle Lorne. Horace said that his brother had always been shy and would probably be happy to live in the basement for the rest of his life. But Margaret thought that Lorne might be able to marry Mrs. Foster from the farm down the way and across the river.

Mrs. Foster was a widow with two little girls, Eleanor and Sadie. Owen and his brothers would have nothing to do with them. The girls came over carrying dolls who drank tea. And Eleanor, the eldest, was a Junior Scientist who didn't believe in Superheroes. Mrs. Foster would visit with Margaret and the two girls would play by themselves in the front room while the boys tore around the house being Doom Monkey.

Mrs. Foster had dusty hair and tired eyes, and didn't look at all beautiful to Owen. But Owen noticed that Uncle Lorne couldn't sit in the same room with her. His face got twitchy and flushed, and he started leaning forward in his seat and rubbing his legs over and over without realizing what he was doing. If she said anything to him he started in his chair and said, "Hahh!" suddenly, as if he'd been smacked. Then he'd get up and say something like, "Just got to… you know," and retreat to his basement.

Uncle Lorne had been in the war and was still nervous, even though it had been over for many years. He'd spent a lot of his time fixing boilers down in the bellies of ships. Since the war Uncle Lorne had worked fixing boilers in buildings, and usually he smelled like a boiler. That's how he was most comfortable, oily and alone. Mrs. Foster brought over some ginger cookies one evening and Uncle Lorne dropped them on the kitchen floor, his hands were shaking so much. Then he stepped on the cookies by mistake, his feet were so big.

Owen knew he didn't want to end up like Uncle Lorne. So he steeled himself about getting used to girls. He didn't want to leave it too late. Every morning when he woke up he said to himself, "Today I will talk to Sylvia." He repeated it while he was getting dressed for school. He would look in the mirror with his comb in his hand and say, "Hello, Sylvia, how are you today?"

It was easy in the mirror. When he was walking down the lane to school he'd look very closely at the weather and practice saying, "It's a pretty day, isn't it?" or, "Kind of cold, eh?" He would have about a mile to practice whichever phrase he thought was most appropriate. By then he would be in the village and close to the cross-street where Sylvia lived. She only had to walk about a hundred yards to the school.

One day Owen arrived at the corner at exactly the same time as Sylvia.

She wore a blazing orange ski jacket and red boots that made her look like fire against the snow banks. Owen fell into step with her. It became blazingly hot. Owen caught her eye and got ready to say, "I heard it was supposed to snow." But when he opened his mouth odd blocks of noise came out — "*spoozzleo*" and then "*h-h-hurditsno*" — and he panicked. He sped up and pretended he hadn't said a thing to her. He was quickly several paces ahead, but then was facing a red light. He considered plunging into traffic. But his feet stopped for him, and then he was trapped, Sylvia beside him again. She did not look at him, and he did not look at her, and it took hours for the light to turn green.

Owen's heart pounded for the rest of the day. "Why was I so stupid?" he asked himself. "Was it so hard to just say one simple thing to her?" Impossible. He was as bad as Uncle Lorne, and would end up living alone in a basement reading car magazines.

On the walk home Owen raced ahead of Sylvia, hoping that maybe she'd be impressed by his speed at least. That night he gave himself a long lecture before going to sleep, and in the morning his mind was full again of the easy things he could say when he saw her.

But he kept missing her for the next several days. When he finally did get to walk beside her again he found himself blurting out, *"Nuttle-rug!"* Then he pretended to be clearing his throat and looked in the other direction.

Owen wanted to ask someone what to do, how to handle this impossible situation. But his brothers would have made fun of him, and his father would never have understood. It seemed, though, that Uncle Lorne might know about this sort of hopelessness.

One night Owen found himself drawn to the basement, where Lorne had retreated. Owen crept down the creaky stairs. Uncle Lorne seemed like a deer in the forest that you had to approach quietly.

He looked up as soon as Owen's head appeared. He wasn't on his cot reading magazines, as Owen expected, but hunched over the old workbench.

"What do you want?" he demanded. He was using his body to shield part of the workbench from view.

"Nothing," Owen said. He sat on the stairs. He was trying to think of how to ask his question, of what his question might be.

After awhile Uncle Lorne seemed to forget that he was there, and went back to work. He was using an old pocket knife to carve a block of wood. Owen couldn't imagine what it was supposed to be. But he sat transfixed, staring at the long, strong fingers, the worn, black, razor-sharp blade, the curls of wood shavings coming off the block and falling to the floor.

The next evening Owen came back. Lorne didn't seem to mind him watching from the stairs. Night after night something odd and beautiful began to emerge from the block of wood. It was a bowl of some sort, with intricate gargoyle faces peering over the rim. It had a rounded bottom now and strange grooves. Lorne carved and shaped, then sanded it smooth. Then he oiled and varnished and polished it, over and over. He muttered to himself sometimes, but rarely said a word to Owen. The silence became something that they seemed to share.

One afternoon Mrs. Foster visited. She brought some more ginger cookies and her hair looked less dusty than usual. Within a minute of entering the kitchen she asked Margaret whether Lorne was in.

Margaret said, "I don't know. He's so quiet that sometimes I have no idea if he's in or away." She turned to Owen. "Go and see if your uncle's in."

Owen went down the stairs. The gargoyle creation was gleaming on the workbench, stained a beautiful dark brown. Owen approached it carefully, looked at it in awe.

"What do you want?" Lorne asked, and Owen whirled around. There he was on the cot!

"Mrs. Foster's here," Owen said quickly. "She wants to see you!"

"*What?*" Lorne sat up with such a jolt that he nearly upended the cot. He ran a big dirty hand through his hair and blew out a hard breath, as if he had just been punched in the stomach.

"I'm not here," he said.

When Owen told her, Mrs. Foster made a little noise, *"O."* Then she and Margaret talked about knitting, and the boys ate ginger cookies.

Some minutes later Uncle Lorne suddenly appeared in the kitchen and thrust the carving at Mrs. Foster. She screamed and put her hand up, as if he was trying to hit her.

"I thought you weren't here?" she said. "What's this?"

He seemed unable to speak.

"Thank you, Lorne," she said. She recovered and took the thing from him gently. "It's an ashtray."

"For your daughters," he said, too loud.

"But they don't smoke!"

Owen could see from the knots in Lorne's eyebrows that he hadn't meant to say that at all, that he'd meant something completely different. But he was so confused, he probably thought he could never possibly explain himself now. So he said, "Hahh!" Then he grabbed back the ashtray and retreated down to the basement.

In the morning Owen found the ashtray in the garbage. He slipped it into his schoolbag. He couldn't bear to think of his uncle throwing out something he'd worked on so hard, something so strange and fascinating. But it also seemed to have interesting powers, like Doom Monkey's Atrocious Hat. The longer Owen carried it in his bag, the more confident he felt.

Then one morning, Sylvia reached the corner just as he was looking up.

"Not so chilly today," Owen said, right in her direction.

Sylvia said, "What?" and he repeated the phrase perfectly. Then they walked together the complete hundred yards to school, without saying another word.

Some days later, when they met at the corner again, he was able to say, "It's very sunny," without getting any of the words wrong. Then the next week he said, "Pretty windy today," and she was able to understand every word.

They never said anything else after that, but it meant that he could walk beside her until the school door. Sometimes during the day she glanced across the room at him.

Then he got an invitation to her birthday party. It was a hand-made card of blue construction paper with a big picture of a cake on it, carefully colored. Inside it said Owen's name, the date and time of the party, and the address of her house.

He put the invitation in his schoolbag, looking in every so often to make sure it was still there. The glory of it burned inside him for days. Now at night instead of giving himself a stern lecture about being a coward, he said to himself, "I'm going to Sylvia's party!"

The party was the following Saturday, but he had to keep it a secret. When the day arrived he watched the clock closely. He knew that he had to leave by twenty to two if he was going to get there at two o'clock.

At one-thirty his mother told everybody to get their coats on because they were driving into town to buy new shoes.

"I don't need new shoes!" Owen said, but his mother said that he did.

"But I can't!" he blurted.

"Why not?"

Owen tried to think of a quick lie but nothing came to him. Soon the whole story was out.

"You're going to a *girl's* birthday party?" Andy asked, and without waiting he and Leonard ran around screaming, *"Girl's party! Girl's party! Girl's party!"*

Margaret said, "You're certainly not going dressed like that!" She marched him upstairs to strip off his old clothes and wash his neck and behind his ears. Then she forced him into gray flannel pants and a scratchy collared shirt with a fussy clip-on bow tie and a blue blazer jacket. Then she made him put on his shiny black shoes which really were too small.

"Girl's party! Girl's party!" sang his brothers.

"Did you get a present?" Margaret asked. "What time does it start?"

"Two o'clock," Owen said. The question about the present took him by surprise. He'd forgotten completely!

"I *did* get a present," he said, to shut everyone up. His mother offered to drive him to Sylvia's house but Owen said he could get there on his own. He didn't want his brothers seeing where Sylvia lived.

He put on his winter coat, which didn't completely cover the tails of his blazer, and pulled his boots on over his cramped shoes. Then he went off in the wrong direction, to confuse his brothers, and doubled back through the woods when he was out of sight. He had his school bag with him, and secretly he'd put in some wrapping paper and tape.

In the woods he wrapped up Uncle Lorne's hand-carved ashtray. Then he ran the full mile to Sylvia's house and arrived only about ten minutes late, puffing and sweating, his feet sore in those tight shoes and the flannel pants rubbing roughly against his legs.

He was the only boy at the party! There were six girls, including Sylvia, all in pink dresses with pink or white tights and shiny, buckle-up shoes. Sylvia's house was beautifully new and clean, with no holes in the roof, and the basement was just like the upstairs. It had carpets and paneling, a leather sofa and a huge dollhouse where Sylvia and her friends spent most of the afternoon.

Owen stayed upstairs helping Sylvia's mother ice the cake. Every so often he would go downstairs and look at the girls. The dollhouse had a doll living-room set and a doll kitchen and even a doll bathroom with a toilet and a sink.

It was as if Owen had come from a different planet and didn't understand the language of these aliens. So all he could do was watch for awhile, then go back upstairs.

He fit in better when the cake was served. He ate six pieces one after another, a personal record. Then it was time to open the presents.

The pink girls huddled around Sylvia while she unwrapped two brand-new dolls, a tea set, a brush and comb set, and a flowery book with blank pages to record her secret thoughts. Then it was time to open Owen's present.

It was pretty heavy, and because he'd wrapped it in a hurry in the woods it almost fell out of the paper by itself. Sylvia turned it around and looked at the gargoyles and the little grooves for the cigarettes. Some of the girls started laughing.

Sylvia looked at Owen for the first time in the whole party and said, "What's *this* supposed to be?"

Owen felt worse than Uncle Lorne in the kitchen with Mrs. Foster. He tried to think of what to say, but now everybody was laughing.

The laughter spread faster than the fire in the ditch, ugly and unstoppable. Why had he ever thought of giving her Uncle Lorne's ashtray?

Owen ran over to Sylvia, grabbed the ashtray, then held it high in the air.

"I am Doom Monkey the Unpredictable!" he announced. *"And this is my Atrocious Hat!"*

He plunked the ashtray on his head and raced around the house. The girls had no choice but to chase him and try to capture the source of his extraordinary powers. Even though they were girls and fast runners, they were slowed down by their long dresses and for hours he managed to squirm out of their grasp.

At the end of the party, furniture was tipped over, there was cake and ice cream in the carpet and on the walls, in hair and on flannel pants and dripping from pink puffed sleeves. The dollhouse had been raided and restored three times, and the Western Hemisphere had been kept safe for civilization.

"Thank you for your wonderful present," Sylvia's mother said at the door when Owen was leaving. Sylvia nodded her head a little bit. She was wearing the ashtray and the gargoyles were hanging upside down. "Did you make it your-self?" Sylvia's mother asked.

"It was made in the canyons before the beginning of Time," Owen said. "And will survive the swirling of a billion storms!"

"Well, it sounds very special," Sylvia's mother said. Sylvia seemed to be holding her breath, waiting for him to go.

"It held a hunchback's heart and has been used by the Emperors of China and Bolivia," he continued. Now that he was brave enough to talk in front of Sylvia, it seemed he couldn't shut up.

"I'm sure she'll treasure it," Sylvia's mother said.

"As long as she dreams of true love and stays away from switchback roads in moonlight," he said, "it will provide extra-terrestrial protection!"

"What?"

It seemed the only thing left for him to do was to propose marriage, but he had no ring. So instead he stepped backwards and fell down on some ice. He didn't look back, but ran the full mile home, as if the hunchback in the canyon was after him, with the Emperor of Bolivia not too far behind.

WINTER NIGHTS

ANDY had a crystal radio that he kept in the closet in the boys' bedroom and took out late at night. It was plastic with a lot of dials in front and wires in the back. When he stretched the antenna to its full height and wired it to the curtain rod, he could usually pick up alien spaceships transmitting from other galaxies. They used whiny buzzing noises to communicate with Earth. Andy would sit by the window listening, hoping to learn the secret of their codes.

Sometimes Owen sat with him and listened, wondering what *Bzzzzz — wheee! — eeeeooo — zzzrrbb!* could possibly mean, while Leonard slept alone in the big bed. The two older brothers would look out the window and speculate as to which star the radio signals were coming from, and whether a total invasion of Earth was imminent.

One night the radio noises changed suddenly,

and the whiny buzzes turned into rapid bursts of electric noise: *Blat! Zappa-zappa! Scud! Krakka-takka! Glurk!* Andy got a pencil from his desk and, using a table of weights and measures found at the back of his arithmetic book, deciphered the following message: "Hilltop! Knock! Zurge!"

"What does it mean?" Owen asked.

"We have to go to the fort," Andy said breathlessly. "They're contacting us!"

"But why the fort?"

"Because it's on Dead Man's Hill," Andy said. The boys called it that because it overlooked the graveyard. That's where they had built a snowfort the weekend before.

"What about Leonard?" Owen asked.

"He'd be too scared," Andy said.

"Maybe not," Owen said. "Remember how he spoke to the Bog Man's wife on Halloween."

So they woke up Leonard and the three of them snuck downstairs and pulled on their snowsuits and heavy boots. Their parents and Uncle Lorne were sleeping, so the boys had to be quiet.

It was bitterly cold, the air so frozen it was still and heavy, and the snow on the path to Dead Man's Hill was packed so tight it squeaked beneath their boots. Andy carried his radio and a big new battery he'd bought with five months' worth of allowance. It had meant missing many issues of his favorite comics, but now that they were about to meet aliens it would be worth it.

The boys knew what flying saucers looked like from watching television and reading the newspaper. But the picture on their television set was often blurry, and it skipped up and down. Most of the stories in newspapers said the spaceships had bright lights, and the aliens used ray guns and wore silvery spacesuits.

"What if they don't like us?" Leonard asked, halfway up the path to Dead Man's Hill. "If they're invading the Earth then maybe they don't mean to be our friends."

"Aliens are superior beings," Andy said. "It's not a question of like or don't like. They just want to meet with some typical Earthlings. It's better that they meet us instead of generals or something." They had seen one movie in which the aliens who were invading were actually very nice but the generals had exploded hydrogen bombs at them, which made them angry.

The top of Dead Man's Hill was perfect for

snowforts because the wind swept big drifts of snow against the rocks there. The boys had simply dug into the side of the biggest drift, and in time the cold air had iced over the insides so the structure was strong. It was cozy inside out of the wind, with the three boys snuggled in together. Andy had brought a candle for light but the little flame added a lot of heat too. This was their own place that they had made together.

Andy hooked up his radio to the new battery and fiddled with the dial. Soon the radio came alive with buzzing and whining sounds, some crackles and burps. Then this came on:

"This is Alan Winter bringing you another edition of Winter Nights, three hours of commercial-free radio."

The voice was deep, slow, soothing and clear. It was the first Earthling program the boys had ever picked up on Andy's radio.

"I have a thought for this night," the voice said, "before I open the telephone lines. Nights like these remind me of a winter long ago, when after the snow and cold there was a day of rain and then more cold, an arctic air mass parked on top of us like a bubble. And all the water on top of the snow froze the world into a skating rink — streets, lawns, parks. The motorists cursed, slipped and slid into ditches, and pedestrians floundered. But on skates it was as if we had wings. From across our lawn and through the park and onto the river — one huge, continuous skating miracle."

The mellow, rich voice came through crystal clear in the snowfort where the boys lay together warm and dreamy.

"One moonlit night," said the voice, "a lot like tonight, if there's room in your imaginations, I remember spreading my coat open like a sail and being blown on my skates through fields and fields. The sky wasn't black so much as a deep purple. And my skates went faster and faster. The trees were all coated in a sheen of ice, the bushes were glossed over, darkly gleaming.

"I think of that night sometimes, sailing on skates across the fields. Riding the ridges, whooshing down the hills. We don't get too many nights like that in our lives. With the air so still and clear, you can look into the face of eternity.

"My name is Alan Winter, and this is Winter Nights. I am waiting for your calls."

There was some music then, and someone called to talk about a problem they were having with hair loss, and then the signal started to fade. It was very late, and there were no aliens, so the boys decided to go home.

On the slope of Dead Man's Hill they tested the snow. Though it wasn't frozen over the way Alan Winter had described, there was a shiny crust on top that could hold them up if they lay on their backs. And, if they dug their heels in and pushed, they could slide along like fish swimming in a lake. Up above them the sky was clear and the stars were clustered by the billions, like cities seen from a great distance. Even Leonard, who'd been getting tired and grumpy, was happy to swim on his back along the frozen snow and look up at forever.

That's what Owen was doing when forever was suddenly replaced by Uncle Lorne's face. He'd come walking up in his big boots, his jacket wrapped around him and his scarf dangling down, the breath coming out of his mouth in clouds of steam.

"What are you kids doing?" he demanded, towering above them. He said he and Margaret and

Horace had been out looking for them for hours. They didn't know where the boys had disappeared to. *"What in God's name are you doing?"* he demanded again.

Owen looked way up at him and couldn't answer because he didn't really know himself. It had started out as one thing and then turned into something else and something else again, and to try to explain it so that an adult could understand seemed impossible. Owen thought of trying to show Uncle Lorne the trick about swimming on your back on the snow, but Uncle Lorne was so big he'd probably just fall through. And the way Uncle Lorne was asking the question, standing there so tall with his eyes so wild, made it all seem foolish anyway.

Swimming on the snow? It had been warm just a few minutes ago when they were on their backs looking at the universe. But now it felt like they were locked in a freezer without any clothes.

On that march home the cold slipped inside the boys' snowsuits and drained away all their heat like a plug had been pulled from the bathtub. Leonard began crying and couldn't stop, not even when Uncle Lorne picked him up and held him inside his own jacket and carried him along. Owen began to shake and shiver, and even Andy started tripping over chunks of ice and odd dips in the path.

They rested for a bit near the bottom of the hill. But a cruel wind had started up, and the longer they waited the colder they got. Even Uncle Lorne looked cold. He'd hurried out of the house without a hat and mitts.

Finally he said, "March with me. This is something I learned in the war." And he sang a little song for them:

Down in the bucket, up on the hill
They were after you then and they're after you
*   still —*
Hey nonny hey nonny
Hey nonny hey!

"That's the song that got me through the war," Uncle Lorne said. "I never sang it to anybody else before. This is your getting-home song. All right?"

Uncle Lorne sang it again. His voice started low and weak, like he really was used to just singing it to himself, but as he got going it became stronger. And when the boys sang, it helped with the walking, and soon they were within sight of the farmhouse.

When they walked in, the house was empty. Uncle Lorne ran them a hot bath, then tucked them in bed and went out again to find Margaret and Horace.

The boys were pretty well asleep by the time their parents got back from their searching. Margaret raced into the bedroom to wake them up and hug them within an inch of their lives. Even though Owen was sleepy, he still heard most of Horace's cursing as if from far away.

In the morning Horace talked to the boys for an hour. He paced back and forth while he talked, and the boys had to stand still and straight and listen to every word. They weren't allowed to ask questions or make a noise. Mostly Horace talked about how upset their mother was and how there would be hell to pay if they ever did anything as stupid and foolish and reckless as this ever again in their entire lives. After awhile he ran out of new things to say so he took to repeating phrases: *If you ever!... What in tarnation?... Tried my best*

Lord knows I have... Cold month in hell before you're ever allowed again...

Margaret stayed in bed late, like she did when she had a bad headache. When she came out and saw her boys, she broke down and wept. It seemed like perhaps the end of the world was coming, and Owen was glad they hadn't told their parents about meeting the Bog Man's wife in the haunted house on Halloween. Margaret thanked Uncle Lorne again and again for bringing them back safe. Then she made sure the boys marched up to Uncle Lorne and kissed his rough cheek and thanked him themselves. Uncle Lorne got embarrassed and said it wasn't anything and they weren't to think about it anymore.

Then Uncle Lorne turned on the radio and they heard the news. Last night a flying saucer had been spotted above the fields outside of town, and Eliot Brinks saw weird lights about one o'clock in the morning when he was sleep-walking and now was missing a cow!

Andy and Leonard nearly erupted at the news, but Owen somehow kept them quiet, and after that it was only the kids who really knew what a narrow escape it had been after all.

THE RAIL BRIDGE

"WHAT would the aliens want with Eliot Brinks' cow?" Owen wondered. It was late at night and he couldn't seem to forget about the invasion of the Earth. He'd taken to going to bed wearing Doom Monkey's Atrocious Hat, just in case he needed extraordinary powers.

"Maybe they wanted some milk," Leonard said.

"They probably made a mistake," Andy said. "They were looking for an Earthling and met up with a cow instead."

"Cows are Earthlings too," Leonard said, and they talked about that for awhile, whether all you needed to do to be an Earthling was to live on the Earth. And if that was the case would birds be Earthlings, since they spent so much time in the air, and what about fish?

"Maybe the aliens captured a bird and a fish and a cow and a human," Andy said. "Maybe they're making a zoo on their home planet."

The boys talked about what it might be like to be in an Earthling zoo on another planet.

"What if they put you in the lion's cage?" Leonard asked.

"Or they might stick you in with an Earthling girl," Andy said. "And wait around seeing if you're going to kiss her."

Leonard said he wouldn't kiss her and Andy asked what if they didn't give you any food till you did? "You'd have to crack," Andy said. "You can't go without food forever!"

Owen thought it might be all right to be stuck in an Earthling zoo on an alien planet if Sylvia were there. He wouldn't mind the aliens watching. Maybe after awhile the aliens would start to look like trees or something in the background.

"I wonder what they'd feed you?" Owen asked. Leonard said it was probably mostly ice cream, because most alien planets are quite cold.

"How do you know they're cold?" Andy asked.

"Mrs. Ogilvie told us," Leonard said. He was in grade one and was beginning to know weird facts. He knew the phases of the moon and why Holland was under water.

"Why would the aliens spend their time on

cold planets when they could go to hot ones?" Owen asked.

"Mrs. Ogilvie said that most of the universe is expanding gas," Leonard said. "And the dinosaurs disappeared because they couldn't adopt."

"Adopt children?" Andy asked.

Leonard hesitated, then said yes.

"Of course they couldn't adopt children!" Andy said. "They're dinosaurs!"

"And that's why they died out!" Leonard said. "Mrs. Ogilvie said so!"

Horace called out then that they were supposed to go to sleep, but Andy had a plan that they should go to Eliot Brinks' barn and see where the cow had been stolen. He thought there might be some clues about the aliens. Leonard said he thought they should just leave the aliens alone.

"That's fine," Andy said. "You can stay here and leave the aliens alone. We'll go ahead, and we won't bother you with any details about what we find out."

"I'm not going at night," Owen said, and they agreed it might be better to wait for a Saturday afternoon so Uncle Lorne wouldn't have to come out and rescue them.

On Saturday the boys set out for Mr. Brinks' barn. Leonard came too because he couldn't stand to stay home alone. There hadn't been any-more reports on the news about flying saucers. But Andy had been picking up some very strange signals on his crystal radio — whirring rattles and odd *glop-glop* noises that he wasn't able to deci-pher even using the table of weights and meas-ures.

Mr. Brinks' farm was on the other side of Dead Man's Hill, across the river and up one more set of fields. Andy figured that the aliens had flown straight over Dead Man's Hill at the appointed time but couldn't see them because they had been in the fort.

"What do you think the aliens look like?" Owen asked. Andy had borrowed a book from the library, and in it were many sketches of aliens made from first-hand eyewitness accounts. Mostly they looked like lizard-men with big, smooth, shiny heads and saucer eyes, and three long fingers and gimpy legs. They were green or silver and had tiny mouths and no eyebrows.

"They probably look like tin foil," Leonard said. "And have two heads."

"Tin foil!" said Andy. "Why would they look like tin foil?"

"Well," said Leonard, "they would have to be light to fly across the universe. And if they were like tin foil, they could change into different shapes easily. So they could be an airplane if they needed to fly somewhere, or a horse if they wanted to walk, or become really thin to slip under doors. And they have two heads," he added, "because they marry their cousins."

Andy said, "What would be the point of being an alien if you were going to look like tin foil and marry your cousin? Honestly!" Then he laughed at Leonard, who tucked his chin into his chest and kept walking into the wind.

"Why couldn't an alien look like tin foil, just because the book hasn't thought of that?" he muttered.

With the cold weather the river was frozen over, but there was deep snow on top of it. When Leonard stepped down from the riverbank he fell up to his neck in snow. Andy and Owen pulled him out and then Leonard refused to cross the river because he thought he might fall through the ice.

"Mom and Dad told us to never cross the river on our own," he said, folding his arms and slumping into the snow.

"Fine. You can stay here," Andy said. "You tell us if you see any tin foil flying around from outer space."

Owen said nervously, "Maybe we shouldn't cross."

"Oh, come on!" Andy said. "This river's been frozen for months! The Empire State Building wouldn't fall through that ice!" Owen thought that even if the Empire State Building did fall through the ice it would still be tall enough to stick out a mile into the air. But little kids would sink and drown.

"They did tell us," Owen said. "And they were pretty angry before."

"All right then!" Andy said. "*Both* of you stay here and look for flying tin foil!" He turned and started walking out across the frozen river. He was the tallest and the oldest but even he was having a hard time in all that snow.

He fought his way about halfway across. Then he turned around and looked back at his brothers, who were standing on the shore watching him.

"It's all right!" Andy called back to them. "You can — "

But before he could finish, the river made a sound like a cannon being fired. *Crack!*

Andy didn't wait. He ran back to shore faster than if a rocketship had been after him.

"What was that?" he gasped when he was safe again. They all watched the river and listened. And after awhile Owen could hear what he hadn't been able to before — the size of the ice underneath the snow, and how hard it was pushing against itself, so that there were little creaks and groans, and long pauses full of strain. And every so often, after it felt like the whole river had been holding its breath for ages, the same kind of *crack!* as before.

"It isn't safe," Owen said, and Andy was silent.

"I guess we'll have to take the bridge," Andy said. He was looking over at the railway bridge that crossed the river about a quarter mile downstream. He started off and the other two followed. There was no path along the river at that section so they had to make their own, tramping through the deep snow, falling every so often. Owen hated the melting snow squiggling down his neck and forcing its way into the space between the tops of his boots and the legs of his snowsuit.

When they got to the base of the bridge they had to climb a high chainlink fence, then crawl their way up a steep, snow-covered slope to get to the tracks and the bridge.

They stood at the edge looking across to the other side.

"There's no sidewalk," Leonard said.

"Of course there's no sidewalk!" Andy laughed. "It's a train bridge."

"But there's no handrails either!" Owen said. It was just flat — two tracks on railway ties with steel girders underneath.

"Why would they put handrails?" Andy asked. "If a train jumps the tracks, you don't think a handrail is going to keep it from falling off?"

Leonard put his finger on the problem soon enough. "We aren't *supposed* to go across this bridge!" he said. "It's not a people bridge at all!"

"It isn't very far," Andy said in a low voice, looking at the snow on his boots. "It would only take a couple of minutes. Besides, there's no other way across, unless we head another mile along the river to the highway."

"What do we do if a train comes?" Owen asked. He looked up and down the track anxiously.

"We either hurry up and go across, or we turn around and go back," Andy said. "It isn't that hard."

"But if we got caught on the bridge — " Leonard said, and his lip began to wobble.

"The only reason we'd get caught is if we panicked," Andy said. "And we didn't panic in the haunted house, did we? We fell in a little trouble but we got ourselves out. Anyway, do you see any trains?"

They looked up and down the track. Owen could see for quite a distance in both directions, and there was no sign of trains.

"My foot would get caught," Leonard said. "Halfway across. And then a train would come and I wouldn't be able to get out of the way."

Andy said, "You just leave your boot in the track and run in your sock feet back to the safe part."

"I don't want to lose my boot," Leonard said.

"It wouldn't happen," Andy said. "It's just going to take two minutes to go across and then it'll be over."

"Maybe we should think about it some more," Owen said.

"On the way home we'll have to cross again," Leonard said. "Look how windy it is."

It was true. The wind was screeching along the river, carrying snow from the surface in slow-motion waves.

Andy said, "It's two minutes! You *have* to go across this bridge, Leonard!"

Andy was usually convincing but Owen knew something had happened to Leonard. He'd stood up to the ghost in the haunted house all those months ago. He wouldn't do just anything that Andy said anymore.

"You didn't go across the river on the ice," Leonard said.

"I tried, and that's the important thing!"

"The important thing is do I want to cross this bridge just so I can get captured by aliens and put in an Earthling zoo? Maybe I just don't!"

At that moment Owen saw a train coming. It had somehow snuck up on them when they were arguing, and now was hurtling at them faster than they thought possible! The three of them scrambled down the bank and huddled against the chainlink fence, covering their ears and eyes, while the train roared past louder than a world war. Owen looked up once and saw a conductor leaning out of a window yelling at them, looking angrier than Mr. Schneider on a bad day. It was the longest train Owen had ever seen, and it took three lifetimes to go past.

When everything was quiet again, Andy said, "I guess we could hike down to the highway and cross the river there."

It took most of the day. All the way along Owen thought about what would have happened if they hadn't listened to Leonard. They would have got halfway across the bridge and then that train would have been on top of them. It was too big and moving too fast to stop in time. They would have had to hang off the railway ties by their fingers, waiting while the longest train in the world roared past. They would never have been able to hang on. They would have dropped off and fallen down—Leonard first, then Owen, then Andy. Maybe the snow on the river would have been deep enough to cushion their fall but maybe they would have plummeted straight through the ice and into the freezing-cold water.

That could have been it — the end of everything. Leonard just saved their lives!

The bridge at the highway was farther than it looked, and the wind picked up as the daylight drained away. The snow just seemed to get deeper and deeper. The three boys hadn't brought any food or water, had nothing to warm them up. But Andy was so concerned about getting across the river so they could get to Brinks' barn that he just kept on going even though they were all tired and hungry and cold. At the highway bridge there was a sidewalk, but when they got to the other side they weren't sure anymore how to get to Brinks' farm. They could go into the woods along the river on that side and head back parallel to where they had been, or they could go on ahead and see if they could find a road. The snow had been so deep on their side of the river that they all thought finding a road would be best.

Along the way Leonard started singing Uncle Lorne's song from the war:

Down in the bucket, up on the hill
They were after you then and they're after you
*   still —*

Hey nonny hey nonny
Hey nonny hey!

Andy added some words:

Caught in a spaceship, flying through the sky,
Creatures with two heads, and tin foil for eyes,
Hey nonny hey nonny
Hey nonny hey!

Owen sang:

Over the rail bridge, almost a train,
Fallin' through the ice, oatmeal for brains,
Hey nonny hey nonny
Hey nonny hey!

It was such a powerful song that it kept the boys going for hours. So it was pitch dark before they knew for sure they were exhausted, starving, near-frozen and completely lost. Leonard looked like he could hardly stand, he was so tired. The tears were freezing against his cheeks and eyelids. He was too little to be dragged across the country on such a day. They all were.

———

Finally they came to a farmhouse. Leonard said, "Let's ask here!"

Andy said in a tired and cold little voice, "All right, if you want."

Leonard knocked on the door. There were lights on in the house but he knocked so softly nobody stirred inside.

"Harder!" Owen said.

Leonard knocked again. This time a big dog started growling and barking and Leonard ran back down the steps. The door opened and the dog burst out and licked Leonard's face so hard he fell down.

"Rex! Down boy! Down!" came a little girl's voice.

They were all amazed. It was Sadie, one of the widow Foster's girls.

Rex was the size of Andy and Owen together, but the little girl put him on a chain like she was handling a bunny rabbit. Then she let the boys in, and they were amazed again.

There inside the warm house, playing cribbage with the other girl Eleanor and with Mrs. Foster herself, was Uncle Lorne, looking as relaxed and easy as if he were part of the family.

COLD FEET

ELEANOR was Mrs. Foster's eldest daughter. She had wild blonde curly hair that fell in front of her eyes whenever she bent forward, and long bony limbs. Sadie was the youngest, with straight reddish hair and bold blue eyes and tiny hands. She was quieter than her sister and seemed to fall in love with Owen that night the boys showed up at Mrs. Foster's farmhouse half-frozen and lost. She made hot chocolate for him and brought him warm socks from her own drawer. She knelt close to him by the fire to help him roast his marshmallows. When she looked at him her eyes went dreamy and Owen's neck started to roast and his hair stood up.

That night Uncle Lorne drove the boys home. Their parents were terribly upset about them being out so late and wandering so far from home, and they didn't even know about the near-disasters on the ice and the train bridge. Margaret stood in the kitchen, which was steamy with the smell of soup that had been boiling for hours, and said that was it, they'd never be allowed out of the house on their own again.

Horace said he was going to give them each a hiding they'd never forget. He went to the cupboard and took out the warped ruler that he used in such times.

"I stole this ruler when I was in grade three," Horace said. He whacked it against his thigh and all three boys jumped. Margaret stood against the counter and didn't look as if she might be inclined to save her sons.

Horace held the ruler up for all of them to see. "What shape is it, Owen?" he asked.

"It's w-w-warped, sir," Owen said.

"And what does that remind me of?"

Owen's lips were trembling badly. But he managed to say, "Of your own mistakes, sir! And how you have to stay straight! And it hurts you much more than it hurts us, sir, to have to beat us, but if you spare the bod you spoil the child, sir!"

"Rod," Andy said.

"Spoil the rod!" Owen cried out.

"Spare the rod!" Andy said.

"Spare the child, spoil the rod!" Owen blurted.

"Quiet!" Horace said in his largest voice. Then he hit himself again on the thigh with the ruler.

There was a loud *crack* and half the ruler flew over the boys' heads and into the soup pot behind them.

Owen couldn't help it. He turned and looked at the soup pot and started to laugh.

"*Shhhhh!*" Horace said. "It isn't funny!" Margaret went over to the pot and fished out the broken piece and said, "Spoil the rod!"

Then they were all laughing. Owen felt it jiggling his skin. He felt like a water balloon inside. He couldn't stand up anymore. He collapsed on the cold kitchen linoleum and wobbled and gurgled with laughter and kicked out his legs in feeble spasms. Soon it was Owen who was so funny, and even Horace started snorting and wheezing and leaning against the wall in limp exhaustion.

That's when Uncle Lorne came into the kitchen and said, "By the way, Lorraine and me are getting married."

"Who's Lorraine?" Owen cried out, and it was minutes before any of them could speak again, they were howling drunk with laughter.

"That's... that's... Mrs. Foster," Lorne managed to say, and then they all screamed even more.

But it was true. Lorne had somehow screwed up the courage to ask her, and Mrs. Foster — Lorraine — had accepted. Not only did it make everything better instantly, but in the weeks that followed, the good news blew like a warm wind and chased out winter early.

Unfortunately, the closer they got to the June wedding, the more often Eleanor and Sadie came to visit with their mother. Margaret was sewing Lorraine's dress, and it was taking forever. They would spend hours in the back room where Margaret kept her fabric and her sewing machine. Sadie grew mushier and mushier around Owen until it was almost unbearable, especially when Andy and Leonard ran around yelling, "Owen and Sadie are getting married!"

One day Owen couldn't stand it anymore. He ran away from all of them and went into the backyard, where he climbed the apple tree and began flying solo combat missions over the English Channel. But even there he wasn't safe. Within minutes his mother was standing under the tree telling him he had to come down and play with Eleanor and Sadie.

"Why?" he asked.

"Because they're your guests!" Margaret said.

Owen wanted to say that he hadn't invited them. He wanted to say that Sadie made him feel like he was buried to his neck in sand with fire ants up his pants. He wanted to say that he couldn't be in love with Sadie, because he was already in love with Sylvia and that was bad enough.

He wanted to say all these things. But he couldn't.

Instead he got down from the tree and went inside where the girls were playing medical emergency in the living room.

"You're looking a bit peaked," Eleanor said to him.

Owen didn't know what she meant, but he nodded anyway.

"You might be in need of scientific attention," Eleanor said. "Take off your shirt."

Eleanor had a certain way of giving an order, and Owen did as he was told.

"Lie down. Close your eyes," she said. "Nurse, pass the instruments."

Owen felt something cold against his skin. Sometime later Eleanor said to Sadie, "I'm going to hand you his liver. You hold it while I stitch down the new esophagus. Don't drop it!"

Owen opened his eyes to see Eleanor kneeling over him with a butter knife.

Just then Andy and Leonard ran into the room to save him.

"Why are you cutting out his liver?" Andy yelled.

"It's just a minor operation," Eleanor said coolly. "We've already replaced his heart with a perfect aluminum one." Then she told Andy to step away because he was getting germs in the patient's body cavity.

Owen thought Andy would push her aside but he didn't. He took a step back just like he was told. Eleanor had very steady hands and her brow furrowed in concentration like a real surgeon's on TV.

"You must remain utterly still," she said to Owen. "If you move even an inch then your replacement spinal cord will be ruined." Owen nodded his head, which made Eleanor throw down her butter knife in anger.

"What did I just tell you? Do you want to be a paraplegic the rest of your life?"

"It doesn't matter," Sadie said. "I'll nurse you *forever*." She mopped his forehead with a damp piece of tissue paper. Then she leaned down and kissed Owen on the cheek.

Owen sat up as if he'd been bitten by a snake and ran away, shirtless.

But he didn't escape for long. A few days later his mother told him that at the wedding he would be walking up the aisle in the church beside Sadie.

"She's going to be the flower girl, and you're going to be her escort," Margaret said.

"Her *escort*," Owen said. It sounded like he'd have to spend the rest of his life following her around.

Another day Sadie asked Owen what kind of house he wanted to live in.

"I hate houses!" Owen said. "I'd rather go live in a cave!"

Then she asked him about furniture, and whether he preferred blinds or drapes, and what pattern he wanted on their dishes.

"We aren't going to have any dishes!" Owen said.

"We have to have dishes," Sadie said quietly. And she reached out to pat Owen's hair, which made him jump back and run to his mother, who said he had to play with her, no matter how gushy she got.

Lorne was also in a bad way. He needed new shoes. But his feet were too big and he'd waited too long to order a pair from the only store that would have his size for sure, the tall man's store in New York City. Margaret said he should try the shoe store in town anyway. And she said Owen needed shoes too so they could go together.

They drove off in Lorne's truck. Spring-green growth clothed the lawns, trees and unplowed fields. The plowed ones were brown and black with mud, and the sky was so blue it hurt the eyes. Lorne had trouble shifting gears, and the old car lurched badly.

"They say that you have to speak and such," Lorne said, his eyes intent on the road.

"I don't want to be her escort," Owen muttered.

"You have to make toasts," Lorne grumbled. He looked across at Owen for a second, then back at the road. "They make you stand up. In front of everybody," he said.

"I don't see why I have to be her *escort*," Owen said.

Lorne made a flapping noise with his lips and shook his head slightly. "Anyway, I'm never going to find shoes," he said.

They couldn't even find the shoe store. Lorne drove aimlessly around the main streets. He rode the brakes hard every time it looked like someone wanted to cross the road or turn into the lane.

Owen suggested they could park and ask somebody, but Lorne had a hard time finding a parking space. He seemed afraid of getting too close to other cars. Finally, many blocks from the main streets, he found a spot with plenty of room.

As they were walking back to the downtown, Lorne said, "You have to say how beautiful everybody is." Then he shook his head. "Not everybody. You have to say what a beautiful bride."

"I don't see why Sadie got to choose," Owen said. "Why she chose me!"

Lorne made the strange flapping noise again.

At the main street they walked past the hardware, the corner store, some fashion shops, the pharmacy. Owen went up to a plump old lady in a fussy hat who looked like she might help.

"Do you know where the shoe store is?" he asked.

"Two blocks over," she said, pointing the direction.

After awhile they found the place. The owner was a small man who wore a suit and tie and had a trim mustache and shoes that shone like mica in the sun. He took out a metal instrument with expandable flaps for measuring foot sizes. When he knelt down he had a hard time fitting Lorne's foot inside the flaps.

"I might have something," he said doubtfully, and wandered off.

"They clink glasses," Lorne said, staring into the mirror at his feet. "You have to stand up in front of everybody."

The salesman came back with a pair of dusty black leather shoes too big for a box. He threaded the laces through the eyelets and dragged back the tongue. Then he knelt by Lorne and reached around to his heel with a shoe horn. Lorne stood up and groaned as his foot settled into the shoe.

"If they don't fit I guess you can't get married," Owen said hopefully.

"These are the biggest you have?" Lorne asked.

"I'm afraid so," said the salesman.

The second shoe went on a little more easily and Lorne paced gingerly, then stopped to look in the mirror. "If I soaked my feet in ice," he said finally, "it might be all right. It's only one afternoon."

Owen chose a pair that tore at his heels and made him make little groaning noises whenever he took a step. They seemed like the right kind of shoes to get for the day your life was about to end.

On the way home Lorne took a side route and parked the truck by a pretty bend in the river where a big willow tree hung over the water. He showed Owen how you could pull yourself onto one of the lower branches and lie very still and look straight down into a pool where half a dozen bass were sunning themselves.

They watched the fish for awhile and then Owen told him all about the problem with Sadie. He talked about her being gleamy-eyed and sticky to be with, and what an awful thing it was to have to walk with her down the aisle.

Lorne listened quietly and when Owen was finished he said, "Hearts are like fish."

"What do you mean, fish?" Owen asked.

Lorne said, "It's rare you can look straight into a heart. You don't find that every day. Even if it isn't the right one. You treat it special anyway. If you don't you might never see another one again."

And they looked at the fish awhile longer before they went home.

At the wedding rehearsal Sadie insisted Owen hold her hand the whole time, not just when they were walking up the aisle. Owen squirmed and sweated and his shoes tortured his feet.

Sadie said, "I think we should have six kids, all girls." She was in a flouncy yellow dress with her hair tied up in flowers. Eleanor was a flower girl too but she didn't need an escort, for some reason. She stood straight and proud and alone. That meant Andy and Leonard could run past at odd times in the rehearsal and make farting noises under their armpits and say, "First comes love, then comes marriage, then comes Owen with a baby carriage!"

"Your brothers are so immature!" Sadie said, squeezing Owen's hand.

On the day of the wedding Margaret insisted that the boys be ready hours ahead of time, and then they had to stay still as statues to keep their clothes clean. But she seemed to be whirling like a cyclone. She fought their hair into place with a brush, scolded Horace about his tie, organized Lorne into his wedding suit and painful new shoes, and phoned Lorraine about the flowers and the catering and her hair and the dress.

As the time to leave got closer they suddenly noticed that Lorne wasn't there. His truck was still in the driveway, but he was gone.

"I think he went for a walk," Horace said. "Grooms often go for a walk on the big day."

"You'd better find him," Margaret said. Horace was the best man and it was his responsibility to make sure Lorne arrived at the church on time.

"He'll be back all right," Horace said.

"If he's late, if he in any way breaks this woman's heart," Margaret said, "then I will divorce you and take the children and go live with Lorraine."

"Why divorce me?" Horace asked.

"Because he's *your* brother!" Margaret said.

The boys were forbidden to go outside to look for their uncle. They had to sit in the living room and not ruin their clothes. They watched the clock turn from a quarter to one and into one o'clock, and then one-fifteen.

The wedding was set for two o'clock.

At twenty after one Margaret said the boys could help their father search for Lorne. So they tore out of the house at top speed and ran to the mud field down the road and into the woods toward the haunted house, yelling at the top of their lungs, "Uncle Lorne! Uncle Lorne!"

But he wasn't there. He wasn't in the bull's field and he wasn't by Dead Man's Hill. He wasn't up the apple tree or down in his basement room. Owen's feet ached badly from all the running and he didn't know if he wanted to find Lorne or not. Either way, if the wedding was on or off, he seemed doomed to be stuck with Sadie.

Finally Margaret said it was time to go. "If he doesn't get to the church on his own," she said, "it's his hanging. He's a grown man."

"Mine too," said Horace gloomily.

When the Skye family arrived at the church at five minutes to two, the parking lot was full and the pews were crowded, but Lorne wasn't there. Andy and Leonard got to sit up near the front where the minister was standing, but Owen had to wait at the back of the church by the big doors holding onto Sadie's squishy little hand. The dress that Margaret had made for Lorraine was cloud-white satin that rustled whether Lorraine moved or not. Everything smelled of flowers and worry.

At a quarter after two Margaret took Lorraine downstairs into another room to wait in private. She told Owen to stay with Sadie by the big doors and keep an eye out for Lorne.

At twenty minutes after two Horace stood in front of the guests and announced that the groom had been delayed and would everyone please be calm for a few more minutes. But Horace himself didn't look calm. He was red-faced and twitchy and sweat was soaking through his suit. Even after he stopped talking, his mouth continued silently opening and closing, as if gasping for air.

"Your father looks like a fish," Sadie said. "And your uncle is ruining my mother's life!"

"Fish!" Owen said, and looked at her. Then he said, "Your *mother* is marrying my *uncle*."

"It doesn't look like it," Sadie said.

Suddenly Owen wriggled free from Sadie's grasp and ran out of the church. She started after him but he didn't care. He just kept running faster and faster and soon he couldn't hear her calling after him anymore. He felt like his feet were bleeding inside his shoes. But he couldn't stop, couldn't rest until he got to the sweet spot by the river. He wasn't even sure he could remember the route but his feet seemed to know, and in awhile he was there. His lungs felt ripped with the effort and his feet were past pain.

Lorne was sitting on the big low willow branch with his bare feet in the water. His shiny new wedding shoes were on the bank beside him.

"Uncle Lorne!" Owen yelled.

Lorne looked at him as if he were an interesting bird squawking by the road.

"What are you doing?" Owen asked.

Lorne said, "I'm trying to get my feet down to the right size. But the water doesn't seem to be cold enough."

Owen wrestled off his own wretched shoes, pulled up his trouser legs and waded in close to where Lorne's feet were dangling. The water felt pretty cold to him. His own feet were in bad shape and the soft mud gave some relief.

"Uncle Lorne, you need to get to the church!" Owen said. "Right away!"

But Lorne stayed still, looking down into the water muddied by Owen's impatient feet.

"Think of the fish, Uncle Lorne," Owen said. "Hearts are like fish!"

It was as if Lorne woke up from a bad dream. He looked at his watch, clambered off the willow branch and took off down the road, leaving his shoes behind. Owen struggled out of the water and chased after him. There was a grassy section beside the road that was fine to run on in bare feet. Owen found he could run better if he fought his tie loose and undid his jacket. He pumped his arms and fixed his eyes on Uncle Lorne's dark back. His uncle was awkward and lumbering but surprisingly fast.

They ran into the church like two barefoot warriors. Lorne was mud-splattered, drenched in sweat, his eyes wild. He said to Horace, "Has she gone yet?" and Horace calmed him down and ushered him to the front of the church.

Poor Sadie had been crying. Owen grabbed her hand and when the music started to play he said, "I can't marry you."

"Why not?" she asked. They were walking down the aisle now and everyone was looking at them. Her eyes were puffy and wet.

"I can't," he whispered. He felt her gripping his hand as if she was never going to let it go.

They were near the front now and Owen could see the minister looking at them. Lorne — barefoot, huffing like a boiler — was gazing over their heads at his bride coming down the aisle.

"We're going to be cousins now," Owen said. "And cousins can't marry. Everyone knows." He tried to keep his voice gentle. He didn't say anything about the Bog Man's wife being blind, or children of cousins maybe having two heads.

They got to the front and Owen stepped to the right to stand beside Lorne and his father. Sadie went to the left to wait for her mom. And all through the ceremony she looked across at him, and he looked at her. He kept his eyes as kind as he could make them, and imagined himself looking into a deep, clear pool.

DEATH'S POCKET

ONE DAY that summer the boys were racing through the woods hunting dinosaurs. Their chief weapons were arrows they had made by stripping the leaves off ferns. The bows were made of alder stalks and kitchen string, and the dinosaurs were terrible but shy beasts, so the boys had to be quiet.

They were creeping in single file, concentrating terrifically, when they got to the clearing by the railroad tracks and saw the crowds. There were black-and-white police cars with their red lights flashing, sirens turned off, and yellow pickets up to keep people away. Andy said the pickets weren't really meant for kids so the three of them slipped through and looked down the tracks.

Owen saw a piece of twisted metal, smaller than a car but bigger than a go-kart. There were policemen in blue uniforms and black hats, and railway workers in greasy train suits, and other men in shirtsleeves and sunglasses.

It was a bright, hot, electric day. Owen couldn't see any train, just the destruction it had left. There was an eerie silence, and the air had a strange taste to it, like something burned in a pan in the morning before you're really awake.

Everyone was talking about what had happened. A man had been on the train tracks with his son on a push-cart, pumping the lever up and down to make the cart go. It was a clear day and sunny but somehow when the train came along there wasn't enough time to get out of the way. Maybe it was because the collision took place so close to the curve in the tracks. Maybe the man looked down at his son at the wrong time. Or maybe the son was pumping on one side of the lever and the father on the other, with his back to the on-coming train.

People wondered why they didn't hear the train coming, but Owen knew from the winter how fast those trains came at you. One moment you could be standing on the tracks looking across the bridge. The next moment you were scrambling down the bank and the train was almost on top of you.

The father had just had enough time to grab his son and throw him off the cart before the train ran him over. Owen looked at the mangled cart. There was no trace left of the man.

Owen had seen people die before on television. Mostly it happened like this. A bad guy would get shot in the heart by the good guy and he'd roll off the cliff and fall a thousand feet into the ocean. Or else the burning building would collapse on both the good guy and the bad guy, but the good guy would manage to roll out from under the flames while the bad guy got his foot caught and screamed while he died.

But this was a different kind of dying. There was that bad taste in the air and the twisted wreckage and so much nothing to look at. The nothing where the train used to be but wasn't anymore, the hole in the bushes where the boy was thrown to safety, the mangled space where the man's body had been.

If the father had time to throw his boy off to safety, Owen wondered, why didn't he have time to gather the boy up and jump with him?

Wouldn't the two take about the same time? Why not save yourself as well as your son?

In a few hours all the people were gone, and then in a few days there was nothing left of the accident except one yellow picket that the police had left behind. The wreckage itself was taken away but the strange burning smell remained.

It felt weird to stand by the tracks and look down at where the wreckage had been and see only a big hole in the bushes and smell that smell. Owen found it hard not to imagine himself flying through the air, watching the train smash the cart and the father and then landing hard in the scratchy bushes with the gravel underneath, the train blasting its horn and the wheels screeching on the rails and the father crying out.

The boys spent many hours that summer staring at a comic book advertisement for a personal submarine. It was made of Styrofoam and dove to a depth of ten feet and could be used for espionage and national defence. It cost $69.95 and came in the mail, but you had to send the money first.

Owen and his brothers tried to figure out how to build one themselves. They had a steel tube and two pocket mirrors that they might be able to make into a periscope. They also had a bicycle chain, pedal set and plastic fan to provide propulsion, and several diagrams of the hull. But they had no Styrofoam, and no idea where to get hold of such a specialized defence material.

"We could try using wooden planks and fill in the cracks with cloth," Leonard suggested. But Andy said the cloth would only keep out the water for a little while, and then it would come pouring in, sinking the sub to the bottom of the river.

Andy wanted to use the submarine to scan the river bottom for giant squids. These squids had been known to swallow ocean liners whole. Owen wasn't sure he would want to come across a giant squid, but Andy said that with the special Styrofoam submarine they'd be able to outrun any squids they came across, so would be in no danger.

"That's why we have to raise some money," Andy said.

But the boys didn't know where to start. Margaret set them up with a lemonade stand in front of the house, but hardly anybody came down the road, and the boys drank most of the lemonade themselves without paying for it. Then Andy signed them all up to do extra chores for money. Leonard set the table every night for dinner, and Andy cleaned out the garage and cut the lawn three times in one day, and raked the gravel on the driveway. Owen swept all the way up the stairs and then down again, and tidied the boys' room so that they could hardly find anything, and scrubbed the bathtub until his fingers hurt.

At the end of a week they pooled their money together and found they'd raised 78 cents toward the submarine.

"How much is left?" Leonard asked.

"Sixty-nine dollars and seventeen cents," said Andy. He figured at that rate they'd have enough money for the submarine by the time they were grandparents.

The boys decided to sell their comic book collection. They had nearly one hundred issues, and many still had covers. They set up a table at the crossroads near the highway and offered them for five cents each, except for the special double issue in which Captain Volatile battled Temptress Serpina for the soul of the universe. That one was

Andy's, and he really didn't want to sell it. But he had brought it along in case a wealthy collector arrived.

Nobody came by until late in the afternoon. It was a little boy in a red baseball cap smacking bubblegum. He leaned on his bicycle and flipped through the enormous pile saying, "Got it, got it, seen it, got it, seen it, read it, got it." Finally he stopped at the double issue of Captain Volatile.

"How much for this one?"

"Not for sale," Andy said, reaching for it.

"It's in the pile," the boy said, holding it away from Andy.

"Just give it back," Andy said.

The boy held it like he might want to tear it in half.

"You don't have enough money to buy that one," Andy said. "Captain Volatile only lasted five issues. This is a collector's edition."

"I can give you twelve cents," the boy said.

"It cost twenty new!"

"And now it's old." The boy didn't look like he was going to give it back.

"If you want to buy it it's going to cost you

sixty-nine dollars!" Andy said. "I don't think you've got that kind of money."

"I don't think you've got that kind of comic book!" the kid said, and before any of them could move, he jumped on his bike and rode away, the double issue rolled and stuffed in his back pocket.

The brothers Skye chased him. Leonard and Owen couldn't keep up for very long, but Andy was a strong runner and madder than a hornet. The boy rode all the way into the village and Andy followed him to his front door, which he pounded on with his fist, even while he was gasping for breath. Owen saw it all from a distance.

The kid came to the door, looked at Andy, then ran back in the house to get his older brother, who had big hands and an ugly smile.

"This is the guy who tried to steal my bicycle!" the kid screamed.

"That's not true," Andy said, his lungs heaving. "You took my comic book!"

The kid's big brother was joined by an even bigger brother, and the two of them pushed Andy against a hedge on the side of the yard. He got punched in the stomach and the nose and bled onto the biggest boy's shoes. For that he got his arm twisted and was sent stumbling to the ground.

Owen wanted to fling himself onto those bullies, no matter how much it would hurt. But he was too late getting there. He and Leonard helped Andy limp home.

"Why didn't you give him the old *one-two*?" Horace asked when Andy had explained what had happened. Margaret wiped Andy's face and made worried noises. Horace made *one-two* motions with his hands.

With the old *one-two* you punch first with one hand, then with the other. If you do it right, like Horace, no one can defeat you. Joe Louis used it and Jack Dempsey and Sonny Liston, and all it took was practice and timing.

In the yard Horace put big mitts on his hands and held them out so that all the boys could practice the *one-two*. Andy was the best at it. He could slam his fists into Horace's hands — *whack! whack!* — and make you want to turn the other way and run rather than get caught in the path of such fury.

"What are you doing to those children?" Margaret asked when she came out.

"I'm teaching my sons to defend themselves,"

Horace said. "Do you want them to spend their whole lives smelling flowers?"

"It would be nice if they had a nose left anyway," she said.

After dinner the boys went back to the house in the village. It was hard not to worry. On the way, though, Andy kept practicing the *one-two*. They got to the door of the house and Andy knocked as loud as he could, with his brothers beside him for support.

The father answered. He was a nasty-looking man with a bent nose and deep black eyebrows.

"Good evening, sir, excuse me, sir, hello!" Andy said nervously. "I just wanted to report to you, sir, that one of your sons, today, this afternoon, sir, stole a valuable comic book from me. And that, also, sir, two other of your sons pushed me into your hedge and punched me in the stomach, sir, and made my nose bleed."

Andy tried to look the father in the eye, but the father was getting so angry that his fists clenched and unclenched, and his lips twitched in a menacing way.

"Jeff!" the father yelled, and then the little boy appeared. He had the Captain Volatile double issue in his hand and seemed surprised that Andy would come back for more punishment. "This kid says you stole his comic book. Is that true?"

"No way!" Jeff started to say, but the father snatched the double issue from his hand and whacked him over the head with it, cracking the spine of the book, which he then handed over to Andy.

"Say you're sorry!" the father commanded. A tiny apology came out of the little boy's mouth.

On the way home the brothers Skye were jubilant, until they looked back and saw three bicycles heading their way, black silhouettes in the dusk. Andy led his brothers into the woods, which they knew better than anybody alive.

The ugly brothers on the bicycles couldn't figure out where they'd gone. The boys listened to them crashing around, their bicycles too clumsy for the narrow pathways, sticks poking into their spokes, roots knocking them off. It was hard not to laugh. The bullies were having such a hard time, while Owen and his brothers were creeping like wolves, keeping their heads low.

They circled back and watched the bullies wandering around lost. Then they headed off in the other direction. Andy had his comic book back. There was no sense fighting if they didn't have to.

The only problem with going through the woods was that they had to cross the railway tracks on their way back home, right at the spot where the accident had happened. It was one thing to smell that burning electric air by daylight, and yet another to have to pass by at night. The hole in the bush where the boy had landed was black now, the murderous tracks glinted silver in the moonlight, and the one remaining yellow picket leaned drunkenly back against a tree.

Owen felt a lump come to his throat, just thinking of what had happened here.

"I *can't* cross those tracks!" Leonard said in a shaky voice.

"You crossed them on the way into the village," Andy said. But that was different and they all knew it. Anybody could cross the railroad tracks on the main road in the sunlight. But now it was night, and this was the spot where someone had died.

Andy said, "You close your eyes and I'll carry you across, okay?"

"No!" Leonard screamed, and both his brothers

said, "Shhh!" because those big kids were still in the woods somewhere.

"This is just two steps — *one-two*!" Andy said urgently. "And then we're home free."

"I can't," Leonard squeaked, and he folded down to the ground, hugging his knees.

Owen walked across the tracks and up the path. "Look, Leonard, it's easy. This isn't like crossing the railway bridge."

"Just two steps!" Andy said, and he stepped across the tracks himself. "Come on!"

But Leonard wouldn't move. He wouldn't even look up from where he was huddling in the shadows.

"We're going without you!" Andy called, and he and Owen turned together up the path.

They had almost disappeared beyond the bend in the path when they heard Leonard's scream. It gave Owen a sickening feeling, like what that father must have felt when he turned to see — too late! — the train almost upon them.

But this was no train. It was the big kids, who had found Leonard, and it was Owen and Andy's fault because they'd left him alone.

There was no question of saving themselves.

They hurled back across the tracks and sprang on the attackers in a devastating *one-two* formation: Captain Volatile and Doom Monkey the Unpredictable working together to push back the forces of darkness! It was true, Doom Monkey didn't have his Atrocious Hat, but they had the power of surprise. They screamed and shrieked like wild animals, and in the darkness the bullies were scared for nearly a minute.

Then they realized who they were up against, and they weren't scared anymore. The biggest brother sent Owen flying into a fern bush, then whirled Andy into some thorns, and the two younger brothers held Leonard by the arms and shook him. Owen made it out of the ferns, only to be tripped and shoved into the bicycles, and Andy got his shirt ripped just trying to get out of the thorns. When he did get out he grabbed for Leonard, but the brothers carried the little boy off down the path and pushed him into a puddle.

Now the three of them were coming back for Andy and Owen. Andy dodged, then punched out — *one-two!* But his fists bounced off the big brother's shoulder like ping-pong balls.

"What was that?" the middle brother asked.

"A puff-ball!" the goon said, laughing.

"One-two!" Andy said this time, right out loud, as his punches glanced harmlessly off the bigger boy's elbow.

"No, I mean it!" the middle boy said. "What *was* that? Listen!" He looked worried. Suddenly there was an odd sound in the night air — a dull, low, menacing moan. The bigger boy stopped laughing and turned to listen.

"Shhh!" both the boys said at once, and Owen thought it would be a perfect time for Andy to hit that bully hard in the stomach.

But Andy stayed still. Then they all heard it again — the sickly, ghostly moan.

"This is where the accident was," Owen said quickly. "We were here. We saw it all."

"You saw the train hit the cart?" the bully asked. His face had grown quite pale.

"No," Owen said. "But we saw where the cart ended up. We saw where the body was. It was right over there!" And from exactly where he was pointing came another ghostly moan.

Those bullies couldn't get to their bikes fast enough. The biggest one hopped on and rode directly into a tree. The smallest one fell off and ran himself over with his own bike, and the middle one went straight into the puddle that Leonard was just coming out of. But they didn't stop for long. All three of them scrambled onto their bikes again and disappeared into the night, leaving the Skye brothers alone and listening for more eerie moans.

"Do you think it was him?" Owen asked when they were walking home. Andy said it probably was.

They couldn't do anything about Leonard's wet and muddy clothes, or about the cuts on Andy's legs and arms and cheek from the thorns, or the bruise on Owen's forehead where he'd landed on the bicycles.

When they got home Margaret said, "See what happens when you encourage the boys to fight!" Horace wanted to know all the details. Did they try the old *one-two?* The boys had a hard time explaining how big those bullies were, how weak their own arms and fists felt when it came time to match strength.

"So what happened? How did you get away?" Horace asked, and they couldn't explain it really, the eerie moaning that seemed to come from everywhere at once.

That night Owen dreamed of the accident. In his dream the sound of the train was exactly like the sound of Leonard crying out. And Owen suddenly understood that by the time the father reached across to grab his son, it was already too late. But at that moment the father did the impossible. He somehow reached into Death's pocket, pulled out his son and threw him safely onto the bushes. He didn't have time to think. The action sprang from his blood.

Owen woke up in a sudden sweat, seeing the crash and hearing the moaning over and over — the same eerie, haunted noise that had saved them from the bullies. He sat up and scanned the darkness to see where the ghost was, and nearly had his heart hammer out of his chest.

Then he saw the odd smile on Leonard's face, lost in sleep as he was, and heard the familiar moaning of his younger brother's ghostly snores.

THE ACCIDENT

AFTER Uncle Lorne married Mrs. Foster, Eleanor and Sadie became Owen and Andy and Leonard's cousins, so they were around a lot.

Eleanor questioned nearly everything the boys did. She said she didn't believe that a Styrofoam submarine could outrun a giant squid and that there were no aliens or ghosts.

"But what about Brinks' cow and the Bog Man's wife?" Andy said.

Eleanor said they must have been optical illusions.

"But Brinks' cow was on the *news!*" Andy said. "And Leonard *talked* to the Bog Man's wife. There was nothing *optical* about it!"

Eleanor listened to Andy's crystal radio and said that the noises weren't coming from outer space at all, they were just radio waves.

"Right!" Andy said. "Radio waves from distant galaxies!" He even got out his table of weights and measures to show her how to decipher the codes, but she wouldn't listen. She belonged to the Junior Scientists' Club, and Junior Scientists stuck to the facts.

Andy said that he thought the Junior Scientists were a bunch of weejees, and Eleanor said it took a weejee to know one. So the three boys left for their fort, which was on top of the garage door that never closed. It was a perfect place to go if you wanted to get away from a Junior Scientist.

Eleanor didn't care where the boys went. She said she would just mix chemicals by herself and invent new compounds to rid the world of disease. She had a Junior Scientists' test tube kit that included many different-colored powders and complicated instructions and a hundred-power microscope to view the wonders of the biological world. She and Sadie opened up the kit on the floor of the garage and started doing experiments while the boys sat up in their fort pretending to ignore them. It was tough, though, because the experiments produced a lot of smoke that made the boys cough and wonder what those girls were going to do next. The Junior Scientists seemed to understand that smoke rises while fresh air remains at the bottom of any room.

Pretty soon Leonard said he thought maybe it would be better to be a Junior Scientist for awhile.

"What are you talking about?" Andy said. "And leave the fort?"

"I think she's trying to burn us out!" Leonard said, and then he disappeared down the rusty cable they used for climbing to and from the fort. The cable was stretched around a pulley, and at the bottom was an old iron box full of rocks. The weight of the box helped keep the door open. Not that you had to worry about the door closing, because it had been stuck open forever.

Eleanor mixed more and more chemicals together. The smoke turned yellow and blue and red and brown, and it smelled like maybe the Bog Man was coming after you, gurgling and fuming.

Pretty soon Owen said he'd had enough of the fort too.

"Why are you being a weejee?" Andy asked.

"I'm not being a weejee. Maybe I'll be a spy and discover what's going on with these Junior Scientists!" Then he shinnied down the rusty cable and joined Leonard and Sadie, who were squatting beside Eleanor and her smoking test tube. The clouds were coming out white now and smelled like somebody dying.

"The power of science," said Eleanor, "is that you can solve any problem that comes before you. This mixture I'm making now improves respiratory ailments and promotes egg production in chickens."

"I don't see any chickens!" Leonard said.

"If there were chickens," Eleanor said, "they'd be laying eggs like crazy."

Andy called out from up top, "I'm going to lay eggs on you guys if you don't stop smoking out my fort right now!"

There was a lot of screaming back and forth, and Margaret came out to tell them to be quiet and play nicely. She was alone with the kids because Lorraine had gone into town on an errand, and Horace and Uncle Lorne were working.

When Margaret came out Eleanor became polite and soft and said that Andy wasn't letting them into the fort. So Margaret ordered Andy to let them all go up. When Margaret ordered something there was an extra wood in her voice. It was as if the words became a baseball bat that she just tapped gently a couple of times, and you knew you didn't want to argue with her.

So Andy agreed that the girls could go up in the fort if they stopped being Junior Scientists and put out the smoke, which they did. The only problem was that they didn't know how to shinny up the rusty cable. Owen showed them how to wrap their feet around it and pull themselves up until they got to the top. Eleanor tried and slipped off and said that she thought her dress was going to get rusty.

"What? So now you don't want to come up?" Andy said. "Our fort isn't good enough for a Junior Scientist?" Eleanor got so mad she grabbed the cable with both hands and kicked her feet wildly, clutched and pulled and clutched and kicked until she got to the top somehow, spitting and saying wild things all the way.

"This is it?" she said when she got to the top.

"What do you mean?" Andy asked.

"You haven't even got anything to sit on!"

"You sit on your behind!" Andy said. There were rafters to look at and the sloping planks of the roof and even two little windows in the floor of the fort that you could look through to see what was happening down below.

"This isn't much of a fort," Eleanor said. "I don't know what you're so excited about."

Owen tried to help Sadie up. She had a hard time gripping the cable with her hands and couldn't seem to make her feet clutch. Owen stood below her with his feet on the iron bucket and pushed, and when that didn't work, he climbed up halfway, then reached back down to try to pull her up.

He was in the middle of doing that when the cable started to pull him up all by itself. It felt magical for a moment, and then it felt like the most horrible thing he'd ever known in his life.

There were screams then, not from Owen but from Andy and Leonard and Eleanor, who used to be up top in the fort but now were sprawled on the dirt floor. The garage door which never closed finally had closed for some reason that might have been science or something more mysterious. But no one cared right at that moment, because Owen was dangling near the roof with his finger caught between the rusty cable and the round pulley.

Andy climbed up first to have a look, and

when he saw the finger really was caught he called down to Leonard to run to the house to get their mother.

It took forever for Margaret to get to the garage.

"What's going on?" she called. Then she opened the door to see for herself, and Owen came down with the cable.

"Did you cut yourself?" Margaret said in the voice that she used when things weren't very serious and kids should stop crying about them.

"I think so," Owen said and held up his finger.

Then Margaret turned and ran back to the house, and all the other kids ran with her.

Owen was left alone. The severed tip of his finger hung down by a strip of skin. There was blood on his hand and the bone showed whiter than the whitest snow.

All at once he felt the pain, and he stood screaming and looking, screaming and looking.

He never knew what took his mother so long in the house. It seemed like she was gone for hours, though really she must have only been looking for her purse. Maybe she really wasn't that long finding her purse, and perhaps a sweater.

Maybe it only felt like an eternity to Owen because he was all alone with disaster.

When Margaret finally returned, she put the tip of his finger back in the right place and had Owen hold it on with tissue paper. He stopped crying then. There was something powerful about tissue paper. Everything seemed better because of it. Owen sat in the front seat of the car holding the tip of his finger on, and all the other kids sat in the back. Andy and Eleanor were crying. Owen knew they thought the accident was their fault. Leonard and Sadie were quiet and pale.

Margaret started the car. It was an old one that Horace had just bought that week for only fifty dollars. He was going to fix it up and sell it for seventy-five, but he hadn't got around to the fixing-up part yet. Still, it was the only car on hand and Margaret started it expertly, then backed out onto the main road and shifted it into gear.

The car stalled. Margaret slammed the steering wheel and started it again. But as soon as she tried to shift it to go forward, the engine quit.

Margaret tried and tried to get the car going. Owen sat still and silent and closed his eyes. His finger really didn't hurt as much as he thought it should, with the tip broken off like that. He held the tissue paper tight to keep everything on and to stop the bleeding. Now all the other kids were crying, and his mother was using evil language.

But Owen knew it was going to be all right. He thought of that day when he was in the middle of the burning ditch, and how he'd had the courage to face the Bog Man when he was trying to save his father stuck on the roof. This could be faced too, if he stayed calm.

Margaret got the car in gear, finally, then drove faster than Doom Monkey on his way to rescue the world. She didn't stop, in case the car stalled again, but honked her horn and waved a lot out the window. After awhile the kids shifted from crying to screaming, but Margaret told them to stay quiet, and there was enough baseball bat in her voice to make it last most of the way into town.

The hospital was made of gray crumbling rock with gray walls and gray-looking people inside. Margaret and the children sat in the waiting area for most of a lifetime. Owen held onto his finger in the tissue paper. The other kids sat still with big eyes, just looking.

There was a large man with a brown beard and

an enormous belly sitting next to them, his eyes hazy. Owen couldn't tell what was wrong with him. But the boy next to him had hurt his arm, and a woman across the way who looked as old as ashes had broken her hip just walking to the door. A vacuum-cleaner man had been right there to catch her, and instead of selling her a vacuum cleaner he'd brought her to the hospital.

And there was a little girl in red shoes who'd been sick since she was born and came into the hospital at least once a week. She knew the names of the nurses and took six different kinds of medicine every day.

Owen's finger hurt all over again when he finally got in to see the doctor. He had to take the tissue paper off and though he didn't want to watch he couldn't help seeing that the tip of his finger looked squished and purply. The doctor washed the wound and had Owen hold the tip back on and said he was going to re-attach it.

"How do you do that?" Owen asked. He figured that because this was medical science there would be a kind of bone glue and maybe a special ointment they could use. But the doctor got out a needle and thread instead.

"You're going to *sew* it back on?" Owen asked.

The doctor told him not to watch, but Owen couldn't help himself. There was the needle going into his skin. There was the black thread being pulled through. The black thread made a stitch pattern that you'd expect to see on some attached part of Frankenstein.

"There. That should hold it for now," the doctor said.

There was an operation later to make sure everything really was in place. When Owen woke up he had a huge plaster cast on his finger. He was alone in a green room with gray curtains around his bed, and the cast looked like something a mummy would wear. Owen drifted in and out of sleep. Margaret came by later and said she'd taken the kids back home to stay with Lorraine. She was going to make Horace buy a proper car and how was he feeling? Was there anything he wanted?

"How long am I going to be here?" Owen asked. Margaret said three days, and Owen told her which comic books he wanted. Then Margaret opened the curtains and wound up his bed so that he could look out the window. His room was up on the fifth floor, and he could see rows and rows of houses and a curving part of the river and half a bridge. He imagined that Sylvia might be walking down the street with her parents for some reason that he'd think of later.

After Margaret left, Owen kept looking and looking, and even when it was starting to get dark he didn't want the nurse to close the curtain just in case.

That night he had a hard time sleeping. He thought again and again of standing in the driveway bleeding and screaming, and sitting so quiet and still while the doctor threaded the needle, and those long moments when the car wouldn't go. He tried to imagine what it would be like to be that little girl coming into the hospital every week practically for your whole life.

Breaking one finger seemed like a lucky thing then. He might have caught all his fingers in the pulley, and Andy and Leonard and Eleanor might have broken their necks falling from the fort, and the car might never have started, and they might have had an accident on the way...

And the Bog Man's wife might not have visited Owen the way she did.

It was late in the night and the hospital was

eerily silent and black. There was no sound except for the drip-drip of a faucet somewhere. It was so late the drip-drip sounded like fists pounding on Owen's eardrums.

Then, there she was, swaying like a curtain in the wind, all in gray.

"You talked to my brother," Owen said, sitting up, trying to see her better.

"How is your finger?" she asked. She stayed in the shadows and when she spoke, the wind blew.

"I broke it," Owen said, holding it up. "It's in a cast."

"I know," she said, blowing cool air on him, swirling her gray dress. She had the tiniest voice. He had to strain to hear her.

"We don't see you so often anymore," she said, and then she blew right out the window, and though Owen tried to get her to come back, she stayed away.

In the morning Owen had Nurse Tudley. She was about two hundred years old. Her voice was sharp and brittle like certain kinds of tree bark, and when she talked, the words snapped out like someone closing a suitcase on your fingers. She brought him breakfast on a tray, then hovered around him in case he got crumbs on the sheets. He was so anxious that he spilled his cereal bowl all over the blanket, which made Nurse Tudley squawk like a crow.

In the afternoon, though, he had Nurse Debbie. She was just barely old enough to be a nurse, and she had creamy skin and playful green eyes and was more beautiful than anyone Owen had ever seen except for Sylvia. She brought a box of toy soldiers and a scale model truck and sat on the edge of Owen's bed and told him about how strange it felt to not be living at home.

"Why don't you live with your family?" Owen asked.

"I finished with my school, and now I have this job," she said. Her family lived almost twenty miles away.

"What about your husband?" Owen asked. "You could live with him."

"I haven't got a husband," she said, smiling. It seemed strange to Owen that someone so radiant didn't have a husband.

"Well, I could be your husband," he said. "Except I'm going to marry someone else."

Nurse Debbie was so warm and easy to talk to,

so Owen told her all about Sylvia, especially about seeing her in the golden light that night at her piano lesson, and messing up her Valentine heart-box, and going to her birthday party. He kept looking out the window for her but hadn't seen her yet.

Later on, when Nurse Debbie brought Owen a glass of apple juice, she asked him what Sylvia's last name was.

"Tull," he said. "Sylvia Tull."

They all came to see him that afternoon — Margaret and Horace, Andy and Leonard and Eleanor and Sadie and Uncle Lorne and Lorraine. Eleanor apologized sincerely for breaking his finger. She said it was all her fault. It was her added weight on the door that had brought it down and sent Owen up and into trouble. Andy lent him his double issue of Captain Volatile battling the Temptress Serpina. Sadie brought him a bouquet of wildflowers she'd picked from the riverbank, and Leonard lent him his magnifying glass in case he wanted to take a close look at the pores on his skin, or the stitches on his finger whenever the cast came off. Then Horace said it was time to go.

Afterwards Owen sat in bed looking out the window, the tiny cars bringing the tiny people here and there. He knew that in every car there was a conversation going on, and he tried to imagine what it was for each of them.

He had a long sleep, and when he woke up there was a note on the table next to the bed. In a girl's writing, in pencil, it said:

Dear Owen,

I came to see you today with my father because a nurse called me and said you were in the hospital. You were sleeping though so I didn't want to wake you up.

Well, sorry you broke your finger.
Have a good sleep!

Sylvia

It wasn't the words so much as the note itself, the wonder of it. That she had come all the way to the hospital and stood there by his bed, watching him sleep. She had pressed her pencil right here and here and here, and written his name and hers, and then disappeared like the

Bog Man's wife. Only her spirit was still there, on the paper.

Have a good sleep! the note said, and it was from Sylvia so Owen took it as a commandment. He closed his eyes immediately and thought of her, as if the thought alone might pull her back and wrap her fingers again around the pencil and create another moment as pure and breathless as this one.

THE EXPEDITION

OWEN stared at the paper on the kitchen table. He was home from the hospital. He had a three-color pencil that he'd sharpened himself, and his broken finger was resting on the edge of the paper, holding it down. He started with "Dear Sylvia" and then stared hard at her name to make sure that he'd spelled it right.

Then he couldn't think of what to say.

It felt like he'd been away for years and had come back a changed person, like those princes of old who would go on expeditions and end up being stolen by pirates and held for ransom. Andy had told him all about it. If your relatives didn't hand over money or jewels or gold, the pirates would just slit your throat and throw you into the sea. In ancient times, according to Andy, the mail was so slow that it could take years just for your ransom note to get back to your relatives, and then they could take a long time saving enough to buy you back. Sometimes when they did get the money together they weren't sure where to send it. So all in all it was probably best if you escaped on your own, preferably stealing the pirates' own ship and then sailing back home in triumph.

There was going to be an expedition that afternoon, and Owen thought he might write about that for Sylvia, but since it hadn't started yet he wasn't sure what to write.

While Owen had been away, Horace had taken down the old front porch, which was rotting. He hadn't gotten around to putting up a new one yet. He was waiting for his friend Wilkes to give him some extra lumber that Wilkes' father had in the family's country home up north. Wilkes' father was holding onto the lumber until the new outhouse was built, but after that, whatever was left, Horace could have it. But the outhouse builder was having a busy season, and anyway his daughter was getting married out east in a couple of weeks. But after that probably he could get around to building Wilkes' father's outhouse, so then Horace could have the extra lumber. As long as he got a truck. Lorne's was laid up, but Horace's friend Alex had a truck that he borrowed from his brother in Norwick whenever his brother didn't need it to court the Willow girl in Limeoak who was going away to stewardess school at the end of the month. So after that the truck could be had for the asking.

In the meantime there was no front porch on the house. The door just opened to outer space and a drop of several feet. The boys loved to launch themselves from the front door at full sprint to see how far they could jump into the yard.

Margaret said absolutely that Owen could not jump out the front door while his finger was broken. So Owen had to do it when she wasn't looking, and he couldn't yell the way Leonard and Andy did when they jumped off.

It felt a bit like parachuting. The boys had in fact spent a whole afternoon making a parachute from an extra sheet that their mother kept in the linen closet for guests. But the guests never seemed to come, so why not make a parachute? They poked a series of very small holes around the edge with their father's awl and tied six feet of string to each hole, then tied the other end of each string to Andy's Ranger Scout backpack, which he strapped on before launching into the unknown. He had to fiddle with it a long time to get the strings the right length so that the parachute could open properly on such a short drop.

They'd nearly perfected the parachute when their mother came by to see what they were doing.

"Where did you get that sheet?" she demanded. Andy turned and leaped out the door, and would have got away except that the parachute got caught on a big nail that had been left sticking out of the doorframe. There was a loud *rip!* as Andy came back down to earth.

Margaret was so angry she jumped right out the front door herself and nearly landed on top of her firstborn son. Instead she landed in the hole that Horace hadn't gotten around to filling in yet. She might have broken any number of things, but fortunately only slipped in the mud, so that she looked even worse than the guest sheet that the boys had converted into a parachute.

At lunch time the brothers sat like silent prisoners and looked only at their cheese broccoli soup. Afterwards they cleaned up without a whisper. Then they set off on their expedition so they could be captured by pirates, then escape with the pirates' own boat, which they could then use to be pirates themselves.

It was a clear day at the end of the summer, in one of the last weeks before school started again. The air was so fresh and bright that there was an extra blue to the sky, almost a gray blue, like it was lined with steel. And even though it was warm in the sun, there was a taste of cold in the shadows, as if winter were trying things out. When Owen ran down the path through the woods and out along the riverbank, he could feel the taste of cold in his lungs, and he knew that summer was just about over.

They had spent days scanning the surface of the river for signs of a giant squid. They had kept their eyes peeled for unusual ripple patterns and had climbed some of the big willows near the river to scan the depths of the murky channels near the middle. They had thrown rocks into the deeper pools near shore to scare the monster to the surface.

The squid had left many clues. There was a broken rowboat sunk in the shallows and surrounded by weeds, which looked like it had been wrecked by a sudden lashing from an enormous tentacle. The boys had found several fish bodies floating upside-down near the shore, completely intact and possibly frightened to death after seeing the beast. And they had also come across traces of inky black scum that might have been left over from the squid's poison. Leonard had started to touch it but Andy held him back. The book of giant squids from the library showed actual drawings of the monsters eating cows and ships and squirting their victims with deadly ink.

But this expedition wasn't about finding the squid. It was a pilgrimage, Andy announced. He said that many of the people stolen by pirates in the old days had started out looking for God.

The boys didn't know how to begin. Leonard thought that God would probably be up in the highest tree on the highest point of land, close to the sky, but Andy said it didn't work that way.

"God doesn't live up in the sky in Heaven," Andy said.

"Of course that's where He lives!" Leonard said. "With the baby Jesus and all the lambs!"

He had learned that in Sunday school. But Andy said that after Sunday school, you learn that the story about God up in the sky is just that, a story.

"It's metaphorical," Andy said.

"What's that?" Leonard asked.

"Metaphor means a story *for* something else," Andy said. "The story about God up in the sky really means that He's everywhere all at the same time!"

"He's *everywhere?*" Owen said.

"He's in the hills, in the rocks, in the water, in the ground..."

Leonard started laughing

"What?"

"Well, if God is *everywhere*, then he must be in toilet paper too! And cheese broccoli soup!"

"And glue!" Owen said.

"God is in worms!" Leonard said. "We don't have to go anywhere to find Him. Just look under a rock!"

"You shouldn't make fun of God," Andy said.

"God is in drain pipes," Leonard said. "God is in nose wipes!"

"Stop it!"

"We could just sit right here and God would come to *us!*" Leonard said.

"God is here already," Andy said. Then, quietly — "He's listening to everything you say."

Owen looked around. There was a bit of a breeze and the grass was bent brown, tired from so much summer. Just for a second it did seem possible that God was in the rocks and the trees and the sky and your old pair of socks, that He was listening to what you said and thought about Him.

"Eleanor says that God is a girl," Leonard said then. "A big girl scientist spirit who made the universe work like a clock."

"That's the stupidest thing I've ever heard in my life!" Andy said.

"Yeah, well, she's older than you and a whole lot smarter," Leonard said. "And you're in love with her!"

Sometimes brothers know exactly what to say to make the ground unsteady. Andy pushed Leonard so hard he went tumbling down the bank and fell into the river in a reedy section where the mud was black and a hundred frogs jumped for cover all at once. Owen could see that Andy felt terrible, but not as terrible as Leonard, who was all wet and black with gunk. Besides that, he'd lost his glasses in the mud.

"What did you have to do that for, you big bully?" Leonard said. Andy went down in the water to help find the glasses. Owen stayed on the shore because he still had the cast on his broken finger and he wasn't allowed to get it wet.

"I am *not* in love with Eleanor!" Andy said as he was groping along the bottom, and just the way he said it, Owen knew for sure that he was. And he knew in that moment that this love business was undefeatable. It captured even older brothers who were strong and brave.

They went over every bit of the river bottom where those glasses could have been. They felt with their fingers and their toes, and made little dives, only to come up empty-handed, their hair and clothes and faces muddy with silt. The water wasn't very deep and there was no current right there to take the glasses away. And although it was muddy it wasn't that bad, so there was no good reason why they couldn't find the glasses. They just couldn't.

"See what happens when you make fun of God!" Andy said. He sat down in the sun and peeled off his swampy clothes. The chill in the air filled his skin with goose pimples.

Leonard said, "You have to keep looking! You're the one who lost them!"

"I'm taking a rest!" Andy said, lying back, trying to get out of the breeze.

Leonard left the water and took off his clothes and laid them out to dry.

He said to Owen, "You have to help me 'cause I can't see very well without my glasses." So Owen took off his clothes and waded into the murky water with Leonard and felt around with his right hand while he kept the other one with the cast on it stuck high in the air so it wouldn't get wet.

Leonard and Andy argued about whether God punished you if you made fun of Him or Her. Andy said God hated it when you didn't appreciate all the things He did to make your life better, like bring the sun up every day on time and make sure there was enough air for you to breathe and breakfast cereal in the morning to keep you alive. Leonard said factories made breakfast cereal, not God. But Andy said where do the factories get the wheat and chemicals to make the breakfast cereal? And Leonard said from the fields and the laboratories. And Andy said where do the fields and laboratories get them? And Leonard said from

Mother Nature, the scientist clock woman who was God.

"So there! You admit it!" Andy said, wading back in the water.

"Admit what?" Leonard said.

And just then Eleanor and Sadie came out from where they were hiding and stole Andy and Leonard's wet clothes and Owen's too, which were still dry.

"Hey!" Andy said, and he started racing after the two girls.

He would have caught them too, except that Eleanor stopped and turned around, and said, "You're naked!" which made Andy stop suddenly and dive into the water.

Then Eleanor and Sadie started to run away, so Andy again called out, "Wait! Hey! Give us back our clothes!"

"What will you give us?" Eleanor asked. Leonard and Owen came swimming up beside Andy then, staying low in the water to keep hidden. Andy said that if the girls would just bring their clothes down to the shore and then go away, Owen would give them his Indian Brave flashlight.

And Leonard said right away, just loud enough so the girls could hear, "But you broke that a long time ago in the haunted house!"

"You idiot," Andy said to him.

"But that's cheating," Leonard said.

"We can't trust you!" Eleanor announced, and she started to gather up the clothes again.

"Wait!" Andy yelled. "You can't just leave us here!"

"Why not?" Eleanor laughed.

"Whatever you want!" Andy said, still crouching in the water. "You just name it!"

Eleanor said it had to be something the boys could give them right there, a fair exchange, and the boys said that would be okay.

"But you haven't got anything!" Eleanor said. Then she whispered something to Sadie, who shook her head. *No.* She whispered again, and Sadie kept shaking her head. Eleanor kept whispering and arguing.

Finally Sadie nodded her head. *Yes.*

"We'll give you your clothes back," Eleanor announced, "if Leonard will give Sadie a kiss!"

"Don't you mean Owen?" Andy yelled.

"She means *Leonard,*" Eleanor said. Sadie's

eyes dropped and Leonard made a low groaning noise that sounded like a frog close to death.

"I'd rather walk home naked!" Leonard said, falling back into the water.

"Shhh!" Andy said.

"I'll crawl home in the mud!" Leonard said. "I'll cover myself with leaves!"

"You're hurting Sadie's feelings," Owen said, and it was true, her eyes were puffy.

"Who cares?"

Andy called back to the shore, "He won't kiss her unless he's wearing his clothes. No naked kissing!"

"That would be all right," Eleanor said, but Sadie was shaking her head now, and she started to walk away.

Eleanor talked to Sadie and Andy talked to Leonard and slowly they brought the two together. Andy whispered, "You don't *have* to kiss her. Just make sure you get our clothes back!"

"Which ones are Leonard's clothes?" Eleanor asked, because by now they were all lumped together and soggy. Andy said to just bring them all. But Eleanor said she wouldn't.

"Just bring Leonard's and Owen's then," Andy

called back, and he explained that with his broken finger Owen was a medical case and needed to get out of the water soon. Finally Eleanor agreed and brought down what she thought were Leonard's and Owen's clothes, leaving the biggest, soggiest things behind.

"You can't look!" Andy said.

"Of course we can look!" Eleanor said, and she seemed so sure of herself that Andy didn't even argue.

"Be quick and they'll hardly see anything," he said to Leonard and Owen.

"No way!" Leonard said.

"Well, just cover yourselves with your hands!"

Owen tried to get out of the water but his feet only took him part of the way and then they stopped. Leonard was the same. Their clothes were right there on the shore but the girls were watching, and it seemed an impossible thing to do.

"Just go!" Andy said.

"I *can't,*" said Owen.

Then something snapped inside of Owen. Suddenly he roared out of the water yelling and splashing, and the girls were so surprised that they just sat there with the lump of wet clothes and got soaked themselves.

Andy too went crazy with the moment and ran like a madman for Eleanor. Even though she was older and bigger, he just dipped his shoulder under her arm and swooped her up in a fireman's lift, then dumped her in the water. Then he turned for Sadie, but she ran away screaming.

"Come on!" Owen yelled to his brothers, and they all made Doom Monkey victory noises as they ran to where Eleanor and Sadie had parked their bicycles. Andy took Eleanor's and Leonard took Sadie's, and Owen ran beside them along the path through the woods, over the railroad tracks that Leonard hated to cross, then along the street back to the farmhouse.

The boys knew all along that they were still naked, but somehow it didn't seem to matter. This was their moment of glory, capturing Eleanor and Sadie's bikes and riding them home in victory, just as if they'd escaped from pirates in the pirates' own boat!

But of course they had no words for their mother when they showed up on the front lawn naked as God made them, mud-splattered and wet, screaming with laughter, with two stolen bicycles. They meant to explain every detail, but there was so much, and words couldn't seem to capture the magic and the glory of it. Especially not after they saw the look of horror on their mother's face that just got more twisted and frightful the more they tried to explain. *Threw Eleanor in the water, Sadie ran away, they took our clothes!*

"I lost my glasses!" Leonard said finally, as if that could explain it. Then Eleanor arrived, soaked and shivering, with Sadie beside her, and the nakedness of the moment was like waking up from a bad dream, only to find that you've peed in your bed.

A THOUSAND YEARS
IN A DUSTY TOMB

I T MIGHT have been the chill from the river water, or the naked run back to the farmhouse, or maybe, as Owen thought, it was the fumes they'd breathed in from the traces of squid scum. At any rate, only a few days after the great expedition, all three boys were sick. They showed the same mysterious spots: ragged red blotches that started on the soles of their feet, then crept between their toes and around their ankles. The spots were itchier than poison ivy, and soon the boys had them on their fingers and ears, noses and necks, and up their arms and down their backs. After awhile the spots turned crusty and broke, then spread to other spots. Then they were everywhere: on eyelids and nostrils and between fingers and inside the boys' mouths.

Margaret and Horace shut them in their bedroom and called Dr. Graves, who was old and bowed and thin as a dried stick. His hands shook even when they weren't doing anything and turned the stethoscope into a silvery blur, cold as an ice cube against Owen's itchy chest.

"Not chicken pox," said Dr. Graves, after he had listened to their coughs and poked their tongues and looked in their ears.

"What is it, doctor?" Margaret asked.

The doctor paused, sniffed, looked at the boys as if seeing them from a great distance. He started to put his instruments back in his black bag.

"Don't know," he said. "Keep them warm and out of the sunlight. Plenty of rest and liquids. Should pass in a day or two. Call me if it gets worse."

Margaret flew into action. The drapes were drawn. The boys were confined to bed and made to drink a glass of warm water every half hour. The spots were so itchy that the brothers couldn't stand it. They writhed and kicked, the agony of one setting off the other two.

"Stop it! Stay still!" Margaret would yell, but it was impossible. Leonard would start to twitch and brush against Owen's leg, which would then need scratching, which would make it itch even more. And Owen's elbow would knock against

Andy's chest and he would start scratching, until the whole bed was a mass of wriggling, squirming, crying and complaining.

"Stay still!" Margaret would yell, and they'd hold themselves rigid like soldiers on parade, but the longer they held, the harder it got. What do you do when everything itches, even your eyelids?

At night they had terrible dreams, which they told one another in the morning in excruciating detail. Andy saw the giant squid oozing its way through a crack in the window, slowly drooling the room full of itchy poison ink. Leonard was chased by a runaway train. Everywhere he went the train followed — jumping the tracks, rattling down the road, climbing a tree, invading the basement, bursting into the closet when Leonard was huddled there, thinking he was safe.

Owen dreamed about becoming the Bog Man. He could feel the splotches growing, joining up, eating away his skin the same way the radioactive bog minerals had turned the mild-mannered scientist into a hideous creature. In his dreams he was an outcast. He lived in the woods in the winter, huddled over a fire with a cup of cocoa and no marshmallows, with no friends and no comic books and no clothes, shivering and alone.

In one dream Sylvia came to him in the woods. She shrieked when she saw him, then ran away when he held out his hand. "Sylvia!" he tried to say, but his voice, like the Bog Man's, was a rasping mass of gurgles and hisses.

Margaret made a burning poultice of baking soda, flaming herbs, cake flour, vinegar and cod liver oil. Three times a day she lathered the paste on each boy in turn, using a huge wooden spoon. They writhed and thrashed in fear but their mother had strong arms and an iron will and there was no escape. Within a couple of minutes this paste hardened into a kind of plaster so that the boys couldn't move even if they wanted to. Hours later Margaret would come with a warm wet cloth and a scraper and work the plaster off, and they would lie free and comfortable for a moment before she scooped on a fresh batch.

For a week they ate chicken soup and lay like mummies buried alive and watched the clock hands turn in their darkened room.

The spots didn't go away all at once. Instead,

like winter, they started to go then came back then drifted off and came back again, on and on like that, until finally, one day, they weren't there anymore.

Owen felt like he'd been dug up from a thousand years of living in a dusty tomb and given another chance at glorious Life. He and his brothers ran wild, up trees and onto roofs, through the woods and back to the haunted house and over to the river and the bull's field — all the great places where Life was and interesting things happened. They took Andy's radio back to Dead Man's Hill and scanned the river again to see if their archenemy the giant squid had left anymore evidence of its evil deeds.

Free again, they did everything at twice the speed. Yet Owen knew that somehow things had changed. First there had been the broken finger, which he still had, and then a thousand years in a dusty tomb, and soon school would be starting again. He began to realize that the time up top, moving around, with sun on your face and the ground moving below your feet and air in your lungs — all that time is so short compared to when you're cemented stiff and the clock won't move and you just have to wait and wait and wait… for what? To be yourself again.

What was it he really wanted to do more than anything else? Now that he had his feet back — his Life — what should he do as fast as possible before something tried to take it away again?

Owen knew as clearly as he knew anything in this world. Time could be short. That's why he couldn't wait until he was grown up before he asked Sylvia to marry him.

But first he needed a ring. He went down to the basement workshop where Uncle Lorne had spent those weeks making the gargoyle ashtray for Mrs. Foster. That was where he found the copper wire and where he carved down the top of the broom handle so that it was about the thickness of a finger. He wound the wire around the wooden finger, weaving the strands, trimming the edges, until he had a ring that any girl would love. True, it had no diamond. He pried one of the spurs off his cowboy boots but it wouldn't stay on the ring, not even with tape. Even so he realized it was a better ring without the diamond — simple and true, like his love, take it or leave it.

As soon as he had the ring, he knew he had to

ask her right away. He couldn't wait until school started. So he began walking into the village to her house. As he walked he fingered the ring in his pocket, and he tried not to think of what words he would use. It would be better if it just happened, like all the great things in life.

He was so busy trying not to rehearse what he wanted to say that he didn't see the moving van until he almost walked into it. Sylvia's mother and father were wrestling with a dresser that had no drawers in it and that still looked like it weighed more than both of them together. Sylvia was playing in the front yard with a purple ball.

"Where are you going?" Owen asked. The moving van gaped open on the street while Sylvia's mother and father strained the dresser up the ramp.

"To Elgin," Sylvia said. "My father's company is moving him." It looked to Owen like Sylvia's mother and father were moving themselves, but he didn't say anything. He fingered the ring in his pocket. Not having anything rehearsed, he had no words to fall back on when it turned out the situation was completely different from what he had expected.

So he asked her if she would walk with him to the river.

"We have a new house in Elgin," Sylvia said when they were walking. "It's a big white one with a swimming pool."

"A swimming pool!" It seemed impossible, such a luxury.

"And a big tree with a swing and a fence so we can have a dog."

"Has it got a haunted house?" Owen asked, and she said she didn't think so. There was no Dead Man's Hill and no woods and no river, either.

"But you're going to come to the same school, right?" Owen said.

"No. I'm going to a brand-new school with room for five hundred kids. And I get to go on a school bus. Every day," she added.

It wasn't fair. A swimming pool and a school bus, and a different school where if a plane crashed into the classroom he'd never make it in time to save her.

"You probably won't have the Bog Man's wife," Owen said then.

"Who?" she said. So he had to tell her the

story, which had to start with the Bog Man and his problems with radioactive minerals. And when he finished telling how Leonard had spoken with the Bog Man's wife in the haunted house and how Owen had spoken to her in the hospital, he had to tell her about listening on Andy's crystal radio at midnight while a flying saucer flew straight over their snowfort on Dead Man's Hill to steal Brinks' cow. And he had to tell about Uncle Lorne and Mrs. Foster and how the wreckage looked the day that father saved his son from the train, and about the weird illness they'd caught from getting too close to the giant squid's poison. And what it had felt like in the ditch when the fire was all around him.

They walked along the ridge by the river, both of them eyeing the water in case the giant squid came to the surface. The river was brown and slow and peaceful. It was hard to imagine a terrifying beast lurking in that water.

Owen worried the ring in his pocket and tried to think of how he could ask Sylvia to marry him. Because now that he really knew her — now that they were walking and talking together — he could tell that she was the only person in the world for him. It was all in how she smiled about Horace stuck in the roof, and wasn't revolted when he explained about the itchy blotches that had been inside his mouth. It was how she hooked her hair behind her ear and then asked just the right question to get him started again. And how she had good stories, too, like when her father hurt his back picking up a tiddlywink and then went around on his hands and knees for the next two days.

And especially, it was in how the time with her rushed by like water in a river swollen with rain. It was the opposite of being trapped in a dusty tomb for a thousand years, and just as good as sitting in the apple tree in the bull's field flying a fighter jet with the fate of the Free World hanging on your shoulders.

They sat down by a big fir near the river and Owen took out the copper wire ring. He handed it to her and she looked at him.

He panicked. If only he'd thought of exactly what to say, then he could have said it, even though his heart was racing and his head was suddenly full of fog. He'd told her every story and every adventure that had ever happened to him.

But now, when it most counted, he had a hard time getting even one word out.

"Is this for me?" she asked. He nodded. How could he ask her to marry him when she was moving away?

"It fits perfectly," she said, sliding it on her thumb. It was too big for all her other fingers, but she didn't seem to mind.

"When you put it on," he said finally, "you become invisible."

"Really?" she asked.

"Except to me," he said. "I'm the only one." What he meant to say was that he was the only one who saw her that night in the winter when he'd been walking back from hockey with Andy and she'd appeared in the window of the school, playing the piano, bathed in light.

But he didn't have time to say all that, because she turned suddenly and said, "Look!"

There it was, out on the river in plain daylight. It was huge and black and moved with the speed of a shadow.

Owen and Sylvia stood together and shielded their eyes with their hands. The sun was suddenly so bright directly where they were looking. There was a terrible disturbance on the water — they could tell by the flashing of the sunlight on the surface — and then just as suddenly as it had appeared, the black menace was gone.

"What was that?" they both asked at exactly the same time, and they raced to the water's edge together. Whatever it was ripped waves against the shore and turned the wind suddenly hot, then cool. It left the same kind of electric charge in the air as Owen had smelled that terrible day on the railroad tracks.

"Was that the giant squid?" Sylvia asked.

"I don't know," Owen said.

They scanned the horizon together but the black menace had moved on, and then it was time for Sylvia to go. He walked her back to her house, where the moving van was full and her parents sat on the steps blank-eyed, their clothes dirty.

"Are you ready to go, Sylvia?" her father said.

"Almost," Sylvia said.

She went in the house for a moment and came back out with Uncle Lorne's gargoyled ashtray.

"I think I should give you back Doom Monkey's Atrocious Hat. In case you need some special powers."

Owen accepted it, and then they both stood silent, not sure what to do next.

Finally Owen said, "Have fun swimming," and he turned and ran down the road, right past Sylvia's parents, who were watching him. Past the moving van, past her house. He ran down the road and out by the river, his head erect, arms pumping, the tears streaming down his face.

Finally, when he got to the spot where he and Sylvia had seen the giant squid, or whatever that was, he whirled like an Olympian and flung the Atrocious Hat into the main channel. It splashed and bobbed and floated and was picked up by the lazy current.

Owen stood watching for a very long time as it drifted away, until it became as small as a speck, bobbing and spinning in the vastness of time, heading for the ocean.